As Zac's car purred silently and powerful ... s of Manh ... e in her lif ... ue urge to rebel and do something *she* **wanted. Which was to eke out another few illicit moments in his company.**

She'd never felt so intoxicated. Heady. The way he'd looked at her, with such thrillingly explicit intent… No one had ever looked at her like that. Her heart still beat a frantic tattoo.

Was it so bad to want a little more of this man's attention? *Yes, because you know very well that if he knew who you were and why you were here he'd have you out of this car so fast your head would be spinning for a year…*

That almost caused Rose to turn in her seat and ask for Zac to stop the car, but they were pulling up outside the club now.

Zac looked at her as the car came to a stop. She was transfixed by his mouth, and she imagined what it might be like on hers. On her skin.

'I'm glad you came with me.'

And ... ns were ...

One Night With Consequences

When one night...leads to pregnancy!

When succumbing to a night of unbridled desire
it's impossible to think past the morning after!

But, with the sheets barely settled, that little blue line
appears on the pregnancy test and it doesn't take long
to realise that one night of white-hot passion
has turned into a lifetime of consequences!

Only one question remains:

How do you tell a man you've just met
that you're about to share more than just his bed?

Find out in:

Look for more *One Night With Consequences*
coming soon!

AN HEIR TO MAKE
A MARRIAGE

BY
ABBY GREEN

MILLS
BOON

First Published in Great Britain 2016
By Mills & Boon, an imprint of HarperCollins*Publishers*
1 London Bridge Street, London, SE1 9GF

© 2016 Abby Green

ISBN: 978-0-263-91616-4

Our policy is to use papers that are natural, renewable and recyclable
produ͏͏ts and made from wood grown in sustainable forests. The logging
and m   the legal environmental
regula

Printe
by CI

Irish author **Abby Green** threw in a very glamorous
career in film and TV—which really consisted of a lot of
standing in the rain outside actors' trailers—to pursue her
love of romance. After she'd bombarded Mills & Boon
with manuscripts they kindly accepted one, and an author
was born. She lives in Dublin, Ireland, and loves any
excuse for distraction. Visit abby-green.com or e-mail
abbygreenauthor@gmail.com.

Books by Abby Green

Mills & Boon Modern Romance

Awakened by Her Desert Captor
Forgiven but Not Forgotten?
Exquisite Revenge
One Night with the Enemy
The Legend of De Marco
The Call of the Desert
The Sultan's Choice
Secrets of the Oasis
In Christofides' Keeping

One Night With Consequences

An Heir Fit for a King

The Chatsfield

Delucca's Marriage Contract

Billionaire Brothers

The Bride Fonseca Needs
Fonseca's Fury

Blood Brothers

When Falcone's World Stops Turning
When Christakos Meets His Match
When Da Silva Breaks the Rules

Visit the Author Profile page at
millsandboon.co.uk for more titles.

I'd like to dedicate this book to the memory of Jimmy Devlin, who was known affectionately throughout the Irish film business as 'Jimmy the Bus'. That was his job: driving a minibus to and from different locations, carrying everyone from cast to crew. He made everyone feel like a VIP, even if it was their first job. He was a true gentleman who oozed an old-world charm and respect for everyone around him—especially women. Men like Jimmy Devlin make it easy to write about larger than life heroes, because he epitomised what a hero is. *Ar dheis dé go raibh a h-anam.*

CHAPTER ONE

ROSE O'MALLEY'S HEART was racing. Her skin felt clammy, her palms were sweaty and she was light-headed. She was basically exhibiting all the signs of heading into a full-blown panic attack, or some kind of emotional and physical meltdown, right here on a closed toilet seat in one of Manhattan's most exclusive hotel bathrooms.

Her surroundings, opulent as they were, were only making things worse. Highlighting the fact that she shouldn't be here. Highlighting the fact that this was *not* her world. She was one generation removed from Ireland, by way of Queens, and to say she felt like a fish out of water was an understatement.

Her reflection in the mirror on the back of the cubicle door showed a stranger. A sleek, soignée stranger. Her normally wavy shoulder-length strawberry blonde hair was all straight and glossy and coiled up into a sophisticated chignon at the back of her head.

Rose acknowledged faintly that she had a neck. She'd never noticed it before now.

Only the bottom half of her face was visible because the rest of it was obscured by a delicately ornate black and gold mask. Her eyes glinted out, looking very frightened and green and almost feverish. Her mouth was painted a garish red. Her cheeks were flushed.

She put the back of her hand to one burning cheek.

Relief flooded her for a moment. That was it: she was coming down with the flu. She ignored the little voice pointing out that they were in the middle of an abnormally warm New York spring and rationalised that she couldn't possibly go out there now—she'd infect all the most important people in Manhattan with her germs.

But just as she was about to stand up, with her sheer black dress shimmering in the mirror, the main door of the powder room opened and some women came in, chattering excitedly. Rose sat back down again, a feeling of futility sinking into her bones.

Of course she didn't have the flu.

But she still wasn't ready to come into actual human contact with anyone. Thankfully she was in the end stall, furthest away from the door. She'd wait till they left.

One of the women who'd entered—Rose figured there were two—spoke in a loud indiscreet whisper. 'Oh, my *God*. Did you *see* him? I mean, I know he's totally hot— but seriously? I think my ovaries just exploded.'

The other woman's tone was dry and sardonic. 'Well, that's just a waste of good eggs. It's common knowledge he doesn't want anything to do with the inheritance his family have bequeathed to any child he might have—he even changed his name to distance himself!'

The friend was incredulous. 'Who on earth would turn their back on billions of dollars and a family name that dates back to the *Mayflower*?'

Rose's insides cramped painfully. She knew exactly who: the most infamous man at the party. *Zac Valenti*. He was here. She'd been hoping he might not be. But he was. And now the palpitations were back.

The women were still gossiping amidst the sounds of rummaging in a bag.

'Everyone thought he was having, like, a breakdown or something after he left Addison Carmichael waiting at the altar, but the man literally rose from the ashes.'

The voices got lower, and Rose found herself straining forward towards the door to hear.

'They say that he's now the richest eligible male in the United States.'

'But did you get the vibe he sends off? Seriously cold— and moody. Like, *you can look, but you can't touch*.'

The other voice turned dreamy. 'I know... Those silent brooding types are so damned attractive.'

There was a squirt of something that sounded like perfume and a derisive snort. 'I think it has a little more to do with the fact that he's a walking gold mine for any woman who can succeed in getting him to be her baby daddy. *He* might not want his family's fortune, but I for one would not say no—and whoever has his baby will have access to the famous Lyndon-Holt fortune.'

As those words reverberated, Rose chose that precise moment to overbalance and fall against the door of the cubicle with a clatter. She stiffened in horror as an awful silence descended over the powder room, and then she heard frantic hushed whispering and the rapid clickety-clack of heels as the women left again.

She sat back on the toilet seat and rubbed her shoulder where it had connected with the door. Hysteria rose. As those women had just pointed out, Zac Valenti was probably the man least likely to father a child, thanks to his well-documented estrangement from his family—the cause of which no one knew. But that hadn't stopped the endless speculation as to *why*. He hadn't even gone to his own father's funeral when he'd died almost a year previously.

After the rift and the death of his father, a new version of the Lyndon-Holt will had been leaked to the press.

It had revealed that if Zac had a child, boy or girl, that child would inherit the entire Lyndon-Holt fortune in lieu of Zac—as long as it carried the Lyndon-Holt name, of course. Many suspected that the details of the will had been leaked on purpose.

So now, if Zac Valenti fathered a child, there would be immense pressure on him not to deny it its rightful inheritance, and the child's mother would have a say in it—including the naming of the child… Something Zac Valenti was undoubtedly aware of and which was probably behind the conveniently leaked will.

Which brought Rose O'Malley neatly back to the reason she was there in the first place. She was here to cold-bloodedly seduce Zac Valenti—one of the most coveted bachelors in the world—with her aim being, however impossible it might seem, to try and become pregnant with his child.

Rose's mind boggled anew at what she'd agreed to. It was only now, a day later, that the panic and fear that had led her to making that decision had faded a little, restoring her to cold, stark reality. And the realisation that she'd made a pact with the devil.

Rose's conversation with her employer, Mrs Lyndon-Holt, was still vivid in her mind—as vivid as the beautifully preserved woman's ice-cold blue eyes.

Zac Valenti's mother had held up the signed contract and said, 'You are now bound by the terms of this agreement, Rose. If you become pregnant with my son's child, and ensure that it will take the Lyndon-Holt name on its birth, it will inherit everything. And once I receive confirmation of your pregnancy, your father will go to a clinic and receive the best medical care for his condition.'

Mrs Lyndon-Holt had continued, 'But if you break the terms of the non-disclosure agreement and reveal these details to anyone, you will be prosecuted with the full force of my legal team. In the event that you *do* have a baby but you don't comply with these terms, I will crush you. Needless to say a legal contretemps between me—' she'd looked Rose up and down pointedly here '—and a *maid* isn't a fight you'll want to engage in.'

The magnitude of what was at stake had hit Rose. She'd blurted out, 'What on earth makes you think a man like your son would look twice at someone like *me*?'

The older woman had stood back and narrowed those calculating eyes. 'A man as cynical and jaded as Zachary…? He'll look. He can't fail to notice a fresh-faced beauty like you. You just have to ensure that it goes beyond noticing.'

Rose came back to the present and looked at herself in the mirror. She didn't *feel* fresh-faced or beautiful. She felt ridiculous, tainted. Garish. With her hot cheeks and the slash of red lipstick. In a fit of self-disgust she grabbed some tissue and wiped the lipstick off her lips.

She couldn't do this. She should never have agreed to such an outlandish plan.

She stood up, galvanised into leaving this place and informing Mrs Lyndon-Holt that she could find someone else to be her sick baby bait. But the reason she'd agreed to it in the first place came back like a slap in the face, and she sat back down again heavily.

Her father. His face full of pain. Pale. Losing hope. Far too young at fifty-two to be facing certain death if he didn't receive the operation he needed.

The kind of operation that was far beyond the reach of an ex-chauffeur and a humble maid, with only the most basic of health insurance.

It was a fact that Mrs Lyndon-Holt had seized upon to use to her advantage, capitalising on Rose's fear and panic. Her father had worked as the Lyndon-Holts' driver until Mr Lyndon-Holt had passed away, after which Mrs Lyndon-Holt had taken on new staff, without so much as a thank-you for years of service. Rose had kept her job, however, and it had been a relief at the time.

Shortly afterwards her father had started to feel unwell, and this had culminated in the diagnosis of a rare heart condition, fatal if not treated.

Rose battled with her conscience. The thought of her father succumbing to an inevitable decline was too much to bear. She'd lost her mother already—far too young. Her father was all she had left. They had no other family in America. And he could be saved easily. *If* he had the operation. The operation that Mrs Lyndon-Holt had agreed to pay for if Rose did this...

She looked at her glittering eyes and hectically flushed cheeks. She told herself that she would make an attempt to find Zac Valenti, but if she couldn't find him—or if she did and he didn't look at her twice, which she fully expected—then she would go. At least she would know that she'd tried her best.

And then she would worry about what to do with her father. But at least she would have given it a shot.

Zac Valenti looked around the massive glittering ballroom from his antisocial location leaning against a pillar at the back of the room. The opulent space shone with a thousand priceless jewels that screamed the social status of their skinny owners like lurid neon signs over their heads.

One woman passed him, literally weighted down with baubles. Her hand looked barely strong enough to carry the enormous ruby cocktail ring on her index finger. Then she caught sight of him and he could see her eyes widen comically behind her elaborately feathered mask as she almost tripped over her feet.

Evidently his own understated black mask wasn't an effective shield for his identity. Zac's mouth tightened. As if he needed proof that he was still the *enfant terrible* of Manhattan, after delivering the biggest scandal to rock the island in decades when he, Zachary Lyndon-Holt—golden boy and heir apparent to become the uncrowned King of New York—had broken up with his family and given up his inheritance.

Not to mention leaving his fiancée standing at the altar of one of Manhattan's oldest Gothic churches in her bespoke Oscar da la Renta wedding dress.

Addison Carmichael, a blue-blooded WASP from the top of her gleaming blonde head and her blue eyes to her toes, was nothing if not a product of her breeding and background—and she was as tenacious as a Jack Russell terrier. Within a year she'd married into a well-known political family dynasty and was currently the wife of a New York senator.

When Zac bumped into her now she smiled at him with only the slightest tinge of malice—his ensuing rupture with his family had diluted her public humiliation somewhat.

He hadn't been worried about causing her emotional trauma—it wasn't as if they'd had a love match. His relationship with her had been as much of a charade as the rest of his life at that time. And he could only be thankful that he'd discovered the ugly truth in his family *before* he'd sleepwalked into a veritable prison of his parents' making.

He cursed silently and corrected himself: *his grandparents making*.

He'd grown up knowing them as his parents until the day he'd found out otherwise, when his world as he'd known it had exploded out of all recognition.

But he'd stayed standing.

And after the shock had passed he'd discovered that all he cared about was the heinous betrayal of the two people who had brought him into this world. A resolve had filled him to honour his real father and mother—not the people who had brought him up as if he was an ill-favoured guest in his own home.

That day he'd had an incredible sense of his own personal destiny rising from the ashes, outside of the weighty yoke of the great Lyndon-Holt name which he'd never felt entirely comfortable with. And so he'd thrown it off, together with everything else bound with that name. And he'd never looked back.

He was determined to make the Valenti name as revered as the one he'd been born with. He owed it to his immigrant Italian father, who'd had the temerity to fall for a Lyndon-Holt princess and in the eyes of her family had sullied her aristocratic beauty...

The fact that a sizeable part of Zac's wealth now came from his new-found career as a hotelier and nightclub owner caused him no little measure of satisfaction— because he knew damn well how much it would enrage his grandmother.

Not to mention the tabloid headlines that had followed his latest nightclub opening, when the supermodel currently being hailed as the most beautiful woman in the world had been papped leaving his apartment late the next morning, looking thoroughly bedded and sexily dishevelled.

So why aren't you returning her calls? asked a snide little voice, which Zac tried to ignore. The sex had been... adequate. But the truth was that their encounter had reminded him a little too forcibly of that feeling of disconnection he'd experienced when he'd discovered the deceit in his family. As if nothing was really real. As if he was a construct...

But he wasn't a construct. He was flesh and blood and very real. And those people could send snide looks and whisper all they wanted—because Zac Valenti was enjoying being a constant reminder that they were *all* part of the façade, just as he had been. A reminder that they were hypocrites and just as liable to fall from grace as he had. Even though he hadn't really fallen—he'd jumped.

He rolled his shoulders in the confines of his bespoke three-piece tuxedo suit, feeling claustrophobic and irritated with the insular direction of his thoughts.

He looked around, seeking distraction.

A flutter of movement in his peripheral vision made him look to his right. He found his gaze resting on the slender figure of a woman in a long, black, backless dress.

She was facing away from him—about ten feet away. So far so unremarkable—Zac had seen women dressed in a lot less in the name of fashion, even if her back *was* remarkably pale and the line of her spine curved temptingly just before it disappeared under her dress. But something about her kept him looking, and as he did, narrowing his gaze, he realised with a jolt of awareness that her dress was seductively sheer.

She moved then—shifting her weight, stretching up slightly as if she was looking for someone in the crowd—and the dress revealed slim yet obvious curves, the globes of her pert bottom encased in black underwear. His eyes travelled up her long, slender back to where strawberry blonde hair was upswept, revealing a graceful neck.

The ends of the black ribbon of her mask trailed in the golden-red strands, and Zac had an insane urge to go over and undo it. Turn her around to face him. He wanted to see her.

He shook his head slightly, as if to clear it, wondering what the hell was going on. Women didn't usually attract his attention without trying.

Then she turned sideways, towards him, and the jolt of awareness became something much earthier and stronger. The black dress teased at an inordinate amount of pale skin, even though she was covered from neck to ankle, and Zac found that he was holding his breath as his gaze landed on her breasts. They were on the small side, but beautifully shaped, pert and upthrust against the fine material.

Evidently she wore no bra, as the dress was backless. With that realisation a rush of heat went straight to his groin, and Zac found himself reduced to the kind of hormonal surges a teenage boy might feel, captivated by his first pictures of naked women.

Her features were mostly obscured by the mask, but he could make out a ripe mouth and delicate jaw. Everything about her was graceful…feminine. She held a full champagne glass in her hand, and from where he stood he could see how white her knuckles were. He realised that she looked uncomfortable, or ill at ease.

He frowned, but just then a waiter passed by and she quickly stepped forward, put her glass on his tray and turned away again. It was as if she'd made some kind of decision. She started walking in the opposite direction, her movements jerky, almost panicked, but she didn't get far because a large group of men blocked her. She hovered uncertainly, craning forward as if to try and see another way out.

Zac's interest was spiked in a way he hadn't felt in a long time—if ever. Because if there was one thing he knew about this crowd, it was that everyone here felt entitled and no one hesitated…over anything. They barrelled through, regardless of niceties. So she was an anomaly, and Zac was suddenly wide awake and deliciously distracted.

Rose was feeling a mixture of sick dread and relief. She couldn't see Zac Valenti anywhere. And right now she just wanted to get out of there—out of this stifling room full of people dressed like glittering peacocks, where she didn't belong, in a dress that made her feel like a call girl.

The stylist Mrs Lyndon-Holt had hired had been like an army officer, barking at Rose to get dressed. When she'd tried to voice her objections the woman had given her a steely look and said, 'I've been given a brief and you're wearing that dress.'

Humiliation crawled up Rose's spine as she thought of the instructions the stylist must have received: *She needs to look good enough to catch my son's eye, but slutty enough to make him believe she's up for it.*

Relief at the thought that Zac Valenti must have left washed over Rose again. She reassured herself that there was no way he'd have looked at her twice anyway. The man took *supermodels* as his lovers, for crying out loud! Not pale and freckled maids who worked in big houses and got themselves embroiled in a deception that was utterly heinous.

Rose was still being comprehensively blocked by a group of men and she balled her hands into fists, determined to push her way through if she had to.

'I sincerely hope you're not planning on taking a swing at the mayor of New York. I'm sure he'll let you through if you ask nicely.'

The voice was deep and sexy and very close to Rose's ear. She spun around in fright and came face to chest with a tall, powerful body. She had to look up, and up again, to see the man's face.

Her heart stopped.

Even the small black mask couldn't hide his identity. *Zac Valenti*. He hadn't left. He was right here.

The mask obscured the upper part of his face, but not the piercing blue eyes glinting down at her. He was famous for his blue eyes. Some called them icy, but right now all she could feel was a disturbing level of heat rising through her body.

Rose's first thought was that pictures could never have prepared her for seeing him in the flesh. He towered over her own not inconsiderable five feet seven inches, and his shoulders were broad enough to block out the room behind him.

His hair was dark golden brown, thick and wavy. He was dark—darker than he looked in pictures—with a hard jaw and a firm and wickedly sensual mouth, currently tipped up sexily at one side.

He oozed the kind of easy charm and grace that came with impeccable breeding and inestimable wealth. He made Rose think of how she'd imagined Jay Gatsby from *The Great Gatsby* when she'd read the book. Aristocratic. Untouchable. Impossibly handsome. A golden being.

Something deep and unfamiliar inside Rose pulsed to life, disturbingly intense. Hot. It struck her: sexual awareness. It was like being plugged into an electrical socket. Her relatively sheltered life with her father, after her mother had died, hadn't allowed for much time to mingle with the opposite sex. Rose had been too busy worrying about her father and the deep pit of despair he'd fallen into.

Zac Valenti cocked his head to one side, eyes sparkling, 'I take it that you *can* talk?'

Rose found one brain cell that wasn't still frozen in shock and nodded her head. 'Yes,' she said faintly, and then more strongly, getting a grip on herself, 'Yes, I can talk.'

'That's a relief.' He held out a hand and smiled. 'Zac Valenti—pleased to meet you.'

His smile had the wattage of the sun at full blast. Rose had to stop herself from blurting out, *I know exactly who you are.*

She took a deep breath. 'I'm Rose.'

His hand engulfed hers. Warm and strong. Slightly rough. He was no soft city boy. Between her legs, her flesh jumped in response.

'Just Rose?'

She was about to supply her second name when she thought of something and panic made her belly swoop. He might recognise her name—she and her father had worked for his family. She thought quickly and said, 'Murphy. Rose Murphy.' It had been her mother's maiden name.

'With a name and colouring like that you can't be anything but Irish.'

Rose was sweating. 'My parents emigrated here just before I was born.'

She pulled her hand back from his. Even though she'd met him now she still couldn't do this. She was out of her depth, her league…her *everything*. Shouldn't men like Zac Valenti have cordons of bodyguards around them? Yet he didn't. He was like a lone wolf. This had been a crazy plan and one she couldn't possibly execute.

She stepped back.

'Where are you going?'

Her tongue felt too large for her mouth. 'I have to… go…' she said lamely.

'Without a dance?'

He extended his hand again and now Rose felt a different kind of panic surge. 'I don't dance.'

'I find that hard to believe—who doesn't know how to dance?'

Someone who grew up watching the girls in her class go to dance classes and who buried her envy because she knew her parents couldn't afford to send her.

Suddenly angry at being in this position, and in this place, Rose said sharply, 'Well, *I* don't…and I really should go.'

She turned away, only to feel a hand closing around her arm, tugging her back. Damn the man. Why wouldn't he just let her *go*? Already she was feeling remorse for being sharp. This had nothing to do with him. Well, it did…but he wasn't aware of her nefarious intentions.

Oh, God. She felt nauseous.

He'd put his hands on her arms now, and she looked up into that classically perfect face.

He was concerned. 'I didn't mean to offend you.'

Predictably, Rose's brain cells were scrambling again under that blue gaze. 'You didn't. I was being silly—I'm sorry.'

His mouth tipped up again in that sexy way. 'Was that our first fight?'

Rose's belly swooped alarmingly. 'You're very smooth,' she remarked dryly, even as she battled surprise that he wasn't more…*arrogant.* She'd had no idea he would be so charming or flirtatious. She hadn't expected to like him.

But then, she thought with uncharacteristic cynicism, if she'd been there as one of the impeccably clad waitresses he really wouldn't have looked twice at her. And she wasn't so naive she couldn't see that underneath the suave exterior were the sharp talons of his own cynicism. A man like him, from a world like this…? His mother was right: they didn't come more jaded.

He smiled, oblivious to her inner turmoil. 'I try.'

Then he slid his hands down her arms, slowly enough to make her breath quicken and her skin prickle into goosebumps. Especially when he brushed against the sides of her breasts.

He took her hand in his and started to lead her towards the dance floor, where couples were swaying cheek to cheek to the seductive tones of sultry jazz.

Rose put her other hand over his and tried to tug free. Aware of a lot of curious looks, she whispered desperately, 'Really, I've never—'

He sent her a look over his shoulder, stopping her words. 'Trust me.'

They were on the dance floor now, and Zac swung Rose round until she was in front of him. She looked at him helplessly. He took her right hand and held it in his and slid his other arm around her back, up high, his hand spreading out over bare skin. And then he pulled her close and she stumbled forward slightly, right into his taut, lean body.

Every thought left her head. Why she was there. What she was there for. Who she was. All she was aware of was how it felt to be held so close to this man, every inch of his tall body, hard and muscled, against her much softer one.

Her breasts were pressed against his chest. His hand was making small subtle movements against the skin of her back. And they were moving, going around in a circle across the floor. Rose couldn't actually feel her feet. She was floating.

Her nipples had tightened to hard points, pressing against her dress. She'd never been so aware of herself as a woman before. She blushed and ducked her head. A finger came under her chin, tipping her face up again. Even in spite of the mask she could see that Valenti looked incredulous.

He shook his head and frowned. 'Are you for real?'

'Of course I'm real,' Rose answered automatically, becoming aware of her surroundings again as she saw a woman gliding past, a condescending expression in her eyes as she looked Rose over from behind her own ornate mask. She tensed in his arms. 'Look, Mr Valenti, I really should—'

He pulled her closer and growled, 'It's Zac. Mr Valenti makes me sound like an old man. And I'm not an old man—yet.'

She looked up at him and gulped. He most certainly was *not* an old man. He was young and dynamic and virile. And she couldn't believe she was in his arms. Even though this had been the exact objective of the evening...

'Do you know,' he said, 'you're the only woman here who isn't wearing one piece of jewellery?'

Rose immediately scrambled to think of something to say under that incisive blue gaze. 'I...er...I'd be afraid of losing something.'

Zac shook his head again in that slightly incredulous way. 'Your jewels aren't insured?'

Rose cursed herself. Of course, every woman here would have insured each priceless jewel she owned to within an inch of its life. However, the only precious jewellery *she* owned was her mother's engagement ring, and that had more sentimental value than real value.

She affected what she hoped was an air of nonchalance and fudged telling the truth with deflection. 'The current trend is that less is more.'

Zac's hand moved then, slowly down her back, his fingers trailing along her spine down to where her back started to curve just above her dress, and her entire body flushed with heat.

He said throatily, 'I couldn't agree more.'

Run—quick, run! said a voice in Rose's head. She was playing a high-stakes game and she was not remotely prepared or ready. And yet, a small stark voice reminded her, she didn't have much of a choice. If she wanted her beloved father to get better. *To live.*

'What do you say we get out of here? Go somewhere a little less…stuffy.'

Zac's voice cut through her troubled thoughts and feelings of guilt. She wasn't a dishonest person and she'd never told a lie in her life. Yet right now she was actively engaged in deceiving this man with every word that came out of her mouth. With her very presence.

But the huge room *did* feel as if it was closing in on them. The heat was stifling. Weakly choosing more time to think about her predicament, Rose said, 'Yes, I'd like that.'

Zac smiled, and it had a quality to it that wasn't remotely civilised. But before she could change her mind he was tugging her off the dance floor, her hand firmly in his, and she had to lift her dress to keep up with him as he cut a swathe through the crowd.

Rose was aware that she could probably just tug her hand out of his and flee, get lost in the crowd and escape through a side entrance, but…treacherously…she didn't.

CHAPTER TWO

ONCE THEY WERE in the vast marbled lobby, the increased flow of oxygen helped to unlock a delayed dose of cynicism that mocked Zac for being so taken by a woman. Yet even this rush of sanity couldn't stop the realisation that he hadn't felt so alive in a long time.

And certainly no woman had ever precipitated this level of arousal. He took her over to a secluded area and as soon as he looked at her he felt any attempt to control his libido turn to dust.

Her cheeks were flushed and her chest was moving up and down rapidly. Cynicism be damned. He didn't want its protection now—he needed to see her. He took his own mask off and threw it carelessly but expertly into a nearby bin. He saw how her eyes widened on his face and his body pulsed with desire.

'Now you,' he said softly. 'I want to see you.'

For a second she bit her lip, and he had the crazy notion that she was going to refuse and walk away and he'd be left with just her name... But then she nodded a little jerkily and took her hands out of his to lift them to the back of her head.

'Wait—' Zac cursed silently. His voice sounded too harsh. Needy.

She looked at him, arms lifted.

'I want to do it. Turn around.'

Slowly her arms came down and she turned, giving him her bare, slender back. Zac had to restrain himself from slipping his hands under the sides of her dress and around to cup her breasts in his palms. Just imagining the scrape of small hard nipples against his skin was enough to send his arousal levels into orbit.

Instead he lifted his hands to where the mask was tied and undid the knot, letting it fall open. She caught the mask in her hand, in front of her face, and Zac slowly turned her around again, a crazy surge of anticipation tightening his gut.

And when she lifted her face to his...he stopped breathing.

She was stunning. But in a way that caught Zac in a different place than when he usually looked at a beautiful woman. She was ethereal...delicate. The faintest trail of freckles sat across her small, straight nose. Her cheekbones were high, elevating her face out of mere prettiness. And her mouth was ripe and full, like a crushed rosebud. *Rose*, indeed. Not caked in lipstick. Ripe for kissing.

Her eyes held him captive. Huge and green, with tiny flecks of gold.

They stood looking at each other for long silent seconds—until Zac realised that they were still in a public place. He'd never lost himself like this...in a moment. As if she was some fey creature in an enchanted wood who'd captivated him.

Feeling more than a little exposed, he took a breath and stepped back. Rose blinked, her long black lashes a contrast to her fair brows. Suddenly Zac wanted to see her in a more contemporary setting, as if that might somehow help defuse this sense of not being connected to reality any more.

He took her hand in his again and started to lead her back to the main part of the lobby, sending a silent signal to the attentive concierge to get his car brought round.

'Wait…where are we going?'

She was tugging on Zac's hand and he stopped to face her. There was something he'd never seen before in the depths of those amazing emerald-green eyes. *Wariness.* Women weren't wary around Zac. They were confident, seductive. Intent on pursuing him.

Not this one. Bells rang in his head, telling him to be suspicious. But the heat in his body drowned them out. He wanted her more than he'd ever wanted a woman. There was something about her that called to a very animalistic part of him.

'We're going to one of my clubs.'

Rose's eyes widened slightly. She appeared almost reluctant, but then she said, 'Okay.'

Zac felt a moment of lightness bubble up inside him. 'Just…okay? You don't care which one?' He did own three of the most successful clubs in Manhattan, after all.

'Should I?'

Her guileless question caught him unawares. Of course she shouldn't. But in his experience everyone always wanted to go to the hottest place. The place that was so hot it wasn't even hot yet.

Zac tugged her closer. 'I'll choose, then, shall I?'

She just nodded. He very badly wanted to kiss her right then, but he'd never indulged in public displays of affection in his life, and he was aware of a million pairs of curious eyes on them. So he drew back.

A discreet cough came from nearby. 'Mr Valenti? Your car is here.'

Zac thanked the man and led Rose outside to where the valet was holding the passenger door open. Zac tipped him and helped Rose into the low-slung silver Falcone sports car.

When he'd got in behind the wheel he looked over to see her staring straight ahead, her hands clenched in her lap, still holding on to her mask. She swallowed, the long graceful column of her throat moving up and down. She was tense.

Something alien moved within Zac. *Concern*. 'I can take you home, if you'd prefer?'

Personally, he would prefer to walk over hot coals than let her go anywhere out of his sight. But he was not about to admit that weakness.

After a few interminable seconds she turned to look at him and the shadows of the car made her face even more ethereally beautiful. She was pale, but determined. As if she'd made some kind of decision.

She shook her head. 'No, I want to go with you.'

Zac felt a disturbingly strong flare of triumph. He ignored it and lifted her hand, forcing it to uncurl, slipping his fingers between hers. A relatively chaste gesture, but one that felt positively carnal when he saw how her eyes dilated. He brought it to his mouth and pressed his lips against her knuckles. A sweet, delicate scent filled his nostrils. Tantalising. Innocent.

His body tightened with anticipation.

'Well, then, let's go.'

Rose was very aware that she'd had two opportunities now to decline Zac Valenti's invitation gracefully and leave. Before this farce continued. But as he'd looked down at her in the lobby she'd been agreeing before she'd been able to stop herself, transfixed by his sheer male beauty.

And what excuse did she have for saying yes just now? *None*.

But, as Zac's car purred silently and powerfully through the streets of Manhattan, for the first time in her life Rose felt a very rogue urge to rebel, to do something *she* wanted. Which was to eke out another few illicit moments in his company.

She'd never felt so intoxicated. It was heady. The way he'd removed her mask…it was the closest she'd ever come to an erotic moment. And then the way he'd looked at her, with such thrillingly explicit intent… Her heart still beat a frantic tattoo.

She'd never had much of a chance to indulge in flirtation with men; her time had been taken up with work and caring for her father. Was it so bad to want a little more of this man's attention?

Yes, because you know very well that if he knew who you were and why you were here he'd have you out of the car so fast your head would be spinning for a year…

That almost caused Rose to turn in her seat and ask Zac to stop the car, but they were pulling up outside the club now, which appeared to be in the basement of a very tall, gleaming modern building.

Zac looked at her when the car had come to a stop. She was transfixed by his mouth, and imagined what it might be like on hers. On her skin.

'I'm glad you came with me.'

And just like that all of Rose's good intentions were blasted to pieces by wicked desire.

He got out of the car and walked around the bonnet, his powerful body sheathed in that amazing suit. He stopped at her door and opened it, which she was grateful for, as she realised that the car was way too fancy and sleek for her to know where the handle was—if there even *was* something as pedestrian as a handle.

When he'd helped her out she became aware of a long

queue of hopefuls outside the roped-off doors of the club. She was also peripherally aware of a flurry of activity between the doormen and someone who looked very officious when they realised who had just arrived. The owner and their boss.

Suddenly there was a cacophony of calls: *'Zac! Zac!'* And Rose was vaguely aware of him putting his arm around her and shielding her as he all but bundled her through a door beside the main one. It was being held open by one of the bouncers.

When the door had closed behind them he turned to her, concerned. 'Are you okay? Luckily the paparazzi didn't get us.'

She nodded, her ears still ringing from the shouting. 'I think so.'

He stood up straight and ran a hand through his hair, quirking a smile. 'I'm more used to people waiting until they're sure they *have* been comprehensively papped.'

Rose shuddered at the very idea of her picture being splashed on the front pages of the tabloids. The thought was horrific. And of course he was referring to the kind of women who were as used to this kind of scene as she was used to a black and white uniform with an apron and to people never looking her in the eye.

But *he* was looking her right in the eye now, and it was very hard to regret being here. Even though she knew it was wrong.

'Shall we?'

He put out a hand, indicating for her to precede him down a narrow corridor, luxuriously carpeted, with dark walls. It screamed sin and decadence, and it was a world away from anything she had ever experienced.

Another spurt of that dangerously rebellious spirit urged

her on. *Just a few more minutes*, Rose assured herself. And then she would go.

She walked ahead of Zac, and she could feel the pounding bass beat of the music coming from all around them. They were approaching a door, and as if by magic it was opened by a handsome young man in a suit. He gave a small deferential nod as they walked in.

She came to a stop inside what was clearly the VIP space, with its velvet banquette seats and gleaming table. There was a railing and steps leading down to the dance floor, which was on the level below. The bottom of the stairs was guarded by another huge bouncer.

The dance floor was filled with hundreds of scantily clad lithe and gyrating bodies. Everyone looked like a supermodel. The local nightclub near where she'd grown up, on Bliss Street, Queens, could never have prepared Rose for this sophisticated spectacle.

She was mesmerised for long seconds, and then she felt a prickling sensation across her skin and looked to see Zac leaning with one arm on the railing, staring at her with a small smile. He was holding two delicate flutes filled with sparkling wine and he handed her one.

She accepted it, hoping she didn't look like a total wide-eyed hick, and he clinked his glass to hers.

'Here's to…new friends.'

'New friends…' she echoed, and took a sip of the golden wine, delighting in the way it fizzed as it slid down her throat. She'd been too nervous to contemplate drinking any of the champagne at the function earlier.

He took her hand with an ease that set her pulse on fire and led her over to the seat—a semi-circular shape around the table. She felt unaccountably self-conscious and nervous now that it was just the two of them in this dimly lit intimate space.

She gestured to the heaving dance floor below and asked a little shakily, 'Is this where you come to survey your kingdom?'

Somewhere along the way Zac's bow tie had come rakishly undone and the top button of his shirt was open. As was his waistcoat. There was space between them, but with his snowy white shirt pulled across his flat belly and one arm spread out along the back of the seat, with a hand resting near Rose's head, she felt as hot as if they were touching. The darkness of his skin was visible through his shirt.

He shrugged minutely, dragging Rose's attention north again. Something crossed his face…some indecipherable expression. Almost distaste. But it was gone before she could analyse it.

'It's a prettier view than the floor of the stock exchange.'

His words were flippant, but Rose detected something sharp. He gave off a blasé air, but she didn't think he was for a second. She could tell that he was supremely aware of absolutely everything going on, and she would guess that there wasn't the smallest thing left to chance.

'I wouldn't know what that looks like,' she replied. 'I've never been there.'

Zac's gaze narrowed on her and her skin felt tight all over.

'So tell me about you. I haven't seen you around before…'

She curbed a semi-hysterical giggle. 'That's because I'm not really from around here.'

Zac frowned. 'But you're a New Yorker?'

Rose took another fortifying sip of champagne. Mrs Lyndon-Holt's cut-glass tones came back to her. *Don't lie—he'll see through you in an instant. Be honest. He won't connect you to here. He was gone before you started working for us.*

Her guts were tangled into a knot. She couldn't believe

it had really come to this. She felt as if at any moment she'd wake up back in that toilet cubicle. Maybe she'd knocked her head as well as her shoulder—

'Rose…?'

She looked at Zac Valenti. This was no dream. He was as real as she was.

Illicit excitement vied with fear and guilt. She swallowed. 'Yes, I'm a New Yorker. From Queens. The truth is…' She faltered for a moment, tempted to blurt the whole thing out, but then the reminder of her signature on the bottom of that non-disclosure agreement told her that she couldn't. No matter what happened.

It was like a slap on the face.

She couldn't tell him the full truth but she could tell him this. 'The fact is that I'm just a maid… I really shouldn't have been at that function earlier, but my boss gave me a ticket. This isn't my world. I'm no one special, really.'

Rose almost hoped that this would be enough to have Zac Valenti recoiling in horror, hastening back to his own kind. But his expression only hardened in a way that she could see wasn't directed at her.

'It's as much your world as anyone else's, believe me.'

Her insides lurched. She hadn't expected him to express solidarity, and she was surprised at the vehemence in his voice.

Then he took her glass out of her hand and put it down on the table alongside his own. He stood up from the seat, pulling Rose with him. 'I want to show you something.'

She balked. She wasn't meant to be prolonging this, but there was something intense in his expression.

Weakly, she said, 'But we just got here.'

He looked at her. 'Do you really want to stay?'

Rose ripped her gaze away from his and looked down over the club—it was spectacular and sinfully seductive, but ultimately it left her cold. Like a beautiful picture with no depth.

She shook her head. 'No.'

A small smile touched his mouth and then he was leading her back the way they'd come—except instead of going back out to the entrance of the club Zac was going through a secret door that led them into a massive and hushed lobby.

A man in uniform jumped to attention from behind a security desk as soon as he saw Zac. 'Mr Valenti, I wasn't expecting you back so soon.'

Zac lifted a hand. 'Relax, George, I'm good.'

'Goodnight, Mr Valenti.' He nodded at Rose. 'Ma'am.'

They were stepping into a lift now, and flutters of trepidation mocked Rose's inability to do what she knew she should: *leave*. Angry with her own weakness, she pulled her hand free and tried not to be so aware of Zac in the small space, but it was hard when he dominated it.

'Where are we going, exactly?'

He looked down at her, his blue eyes bright enough to hurt. 'Trust me.'

He'd said that twice now. This man was a complete stranger to her, and yet she was allowing him to lead her astray as easily as if she was a lemming going over a cliff.

Irritation with herself made her say testily, 'I barely know you.'

He leant back against the wall of the elevator, hands in his pockets, exuding louche arrogance, and arched an amused brow. 'Do you *really* think I'd have alerted a witness to the fact that I'm with you if I was intent on some wicked deed?'

Heat bloomed deep inside Rose at the look in his eyes that told her his head was indeed filled with all sorts of delicious wickedness. But *she* was the one who was really being wicked here.

The bell pinged then, and Zac straightened up and said, 'I promise to deliver you straight back to George if you don't want to stay...'

She was just thinking *Stay where?* when the doors slid open and she gasped.

Rose stepped out and blinked hard. It was like stepping through the back of a wardrobe into Narnia. If Narnia was under a star-filled Manhattan sky.

It was a garden, with some parts like a wild meadow and others like a very ordered English garden. Rose didn't even realise she'd walked so far until she saw she was standing right in the middle of a huge green space on a central paved walkway.

The dark smudge of Central Park was visible in the distance and lights twinkled from the buildings around them, giving the illusion of being suspended in mid-air, amongst the tall structures.

'This is the most beautiful thing I've ever seen,' she breathed in awe, thinking poignantly of her mother, who had loved gardens.

'It took some time to perfect.'

She looked at Zac as understanding dawned. 'You built this...? How long did it take?'

Five years, to be precise. But Zac didn't say that. He led Rose over to an elevated terrace that looked in the opposite direction.

When they were at the railing he guided her in front of him and placed his arms around hers, his hands resting on either side of her on the rail. Trapping her against him.

He gritted his jaw but his body reacted helplessly, rising to the temptation of the provocation of her buttocks against him.

She was tense. Again, not a reaction he was used to with women, who were generally all too eager to capitalise on his exclusive interest.

In a bid to slow the blood rushing to his crotch, he leant forward slightly and pointed. 'See over there? That's the Rockefeller Center.'

Her head moved to the left, away from Zac, and he struggled not to press his mouth to her bared neck. The urge to bite that pale skin was almost overwhelming. With some dark humour he figured that he knew how vampires felt. Her scent was light and floral. Sweet. Sexy. Intoxicating.

Curbing his desire, he pointed again to the right. 'That's Carnegie Hall. Times Square is just beyond.'

Rose's face was close to Zac's now, turning to follow the direction of his finger. She was trembling very lightly, her hands in a white-knuckled grip on the railing.

Her voice was husky. 'Is this what you do to impress women?' She huffed a little laugh. 'I have to admit, it's working.'

Zac stood up straight, surprised at the immediate indignation he felt. He was no angel, but he resented the insinuation that this was a well-worn routine.

He turned Rose to face him. Her green eyes were huge. Luminous. 'I don't bring *any* women up here. You're the first.'

Rose looked up at one of Manhattan's most desirable men, standing against the backdrop of a glittering city that he could command to do his will with a mere click of his fingers. It was the kind of view most New Yorkers were only lucky enough to see if they queued up to climb the

Empire State building or similar tourist attractions. And it was in his backyard.

It was all so unexpected…and especially this amazing, incongruous and wondrous slice of greenery that he'd created, which was so magical.

She desperately wanted to believe he was just spinning her a line, because that would help her feel disgusted with herself—and him. And that would give her the impetus she needed to leave, and walk away.

But she couldn't move—treacherously. Was he lying? But why would he lie? As if he needed to impress a woman with a mere *garden*—even if it did soar magically above one of the most vibrant cities in the world. The thought that she really might be the first woman he'd brought here was a little overwhelming and ultimately too seductive to resist.

As if sensing her vacillation, her desire to believe him, Zac cupped her jaw, his fingers light on the back of her neck. 'I've never met anyone like you, Rose. You're different…'

She swallowed down an urge to giggle at his understatement. 'You can say that again.'

Her heart thumped erratically against her breastbone. She wasn't aware of their surroundings any more, only of the fact that he was looking at her as if she truly was… something special.

For all that she had a soft, romantic core that she didn't show to the world, and in spite of her unfashionable lack of experience, she was street-smart and had a healthy cynicism about men and love.

You couldn't be a woman living in the twenty-first century in New York and *not* know that fairy tales really only existed in movies or books. But Zac Valenti was dangerous, because he made her yearn for something that she'd seen between her parents. He made her think that perhaps the fairy tale was possible...

Zac's head ducked at that moment, and before Rose could finish her thought his mouth was settling over hers and words and thoughts fused into one blinding white flash of heat.

Fairy tales were the last thing on Rose's mind now, under the masterful and expert touch of Zac's hard mouth. Carnality—that was on her mind as heat raced through her bloodstream and into every erogenous zone, breathing fire into her nerve endings until they were tingling and jumping.

He'd cupped both hands around her face now, and his tongue was sliding past her shamefully weak and shy resistance to stroke and explore, urging her mouth open, compelling her to accept him.

The sheer power of his kiss was breathtaking, and so was the arrogance with which he calmly and methodically went about stealing her sanity.

Rose only realised she was clinging on to his waist when her fingers encountered hard, unyielding muscle. The kiss was hard, yet soft, and rough enough to send a thrill through her. She was gasping when Zac left her mouth to kiss along her jawline.

He pulled her closer, one arm wrapped so far around her back that his hand slid under her dress, across her bare skin. His fingers were tantalisingly close to her breast. His other hand undid her hair and Rose could feel it fall down and his fingers exploring, threading through the silken strands, cupping her skull.

Rose let her head fall back, giving him better access to her jaw and neck, and his mouth blazed a trail of fire across her skin.

Dimly, she knew she should be making some kind of

effort to stop this, but the temptation to go deeper into this new world of sensations was too great to resist. She felt powerful, feminine. Desirable.

Zac lifted his head from her neck and Rose looked up, dazed. Her breath was coming fast and harsh and her breasts were moving against his chest, making her aware of how hard her nipples were.

His eyes burned a bright blue, his cheeks were flushed, and a lock of hair flopped onto his brow. It made her feel curiously tender amidst the tumult rushing through her system.

Then he subtly moved his hips, and the bold thrust of his erection told her far more starkly just how real this was. And his words.

'I want you.'

His voice sounded guttural and almost coarse. It should have jarred against this beautiful and civilised backdrop, but it didn't. Because high on this terrace, overlooking the shining city, Rose felt disconnected from everything but this moment and this man. His coarseness and his arousal resonated deep inside her.

She struggled to put some kind of brake on this crazy, all-consuming urge just to say *yes*. She put her hands on his chest, forced some space between them. She felt undone, with her hair around her face and her mouth swollen from his kisses.

'I don't…do this.' The words were a hopelessly ineffectual attempt to articulate her confusion.

Zac finally—mercifully—straightened and moved back a little too. His mouth twisted. 'Would you believe me if I said I don't do this either?'

The space between them finally restored some of Rose's functioning brain cells. Because she knew very well that Zac might not have brought a woman up to this garden, but he *did* do this. Very frequently, if the gossip columns were to be believed.

She stepped back, burningly aware of the telltale dampness between her legs. She folded her arms across her chest, residual heat making her feel prickly. 'You might not do this *here*, but you do seduce women elsewhere. So, no, I don't believe you when you say you "don't do this".'

His expression hardened, giving Rose an insight into another, more intimidating side of this man that she hadn't seen yet.

'I'm not a monk, but I'm not a player. Women know where they stand with me, and when I take a lover I'm faithful to her for as long as it lasts. We have fun and then we move on. I'm not into commitment.'

I'm not into commitment. Rose hated the swoop of her insides to hear it articulated so baldly.

She lifted her chin. 'And is that what you're offering here?' She cursed herself, feeling impossibly gauche. Show the girl from Queens a cool club and an even cooler secret rooftop garden and she'd be eating out of your hand like a bird. Throw in one of the world's most gorgeous and eligible bachelors and she'd be ready to do a lot more.

But that's why you're here, a snide voice reminded her. So who was she to judge him? He didn't deserve her judgment!

Rose whirled away from that penetrating blue gaze before he might see something, her stomach in knots and her brain freezing at the thought that what she'd been sent to accomplish had so nearly become a reality...

Zac cursed behind her, and even though she'd only known him a few hours she could already imagine him raking a hand through his hair.

'I'm sorry,' she said frigidly. 'No doubt you're used to a more...sophisticated response.'

It's not that,' he grated harshly. 'I'm angry with myself. I'm not in the habit of propositioning women within hours of meeting them.'

Slowly she turned around to face him again. His face was unreadable but his eyes glowed. The knots in her belly loosened. She didn't doubt his sincerity. This man was proud. Prouder than anyone she'd ever met.

She could at least be honest about this. 'I don't even know you.'

Zac's mouth quirked with that easy sexiness and he leant back against the railing, his hands behind him. Lord and master of all he surveyed. Power and privilege sitting easily on his shoulders.

'Most people assume they know me.'

Rose felt shy and lifted a shoulder in a half-shrug. 'That's understandable, I guess.'

He turned and faced forward again, leaning on the railing. He looked out over the view for a long moment, and then he looked sideways at her. His voice had a resigned quality. 'What do you say to a coffee and then I'll arrange for my driver to take you home?'

The rush of disappointment was acute, even though Rose knew she should be welcoming it. Zac was obviously bored rigid. But even that thought couldn't compel her do the right thing when she had the chance. She longed for a few last seconds basking in his golden aura.

'Okay, that sounds good.'

She told herself that she welcomed the chance to sober up, even though she'd hardly even drunk. She felt drunk though—drunk on this man.

Zac just nodded, showing no discernible emotion at her acquiescence, and she preceded him back through the garden.

He directed her to a different door this time, not back

to the lift. He opened it and indicated for Rose to go first. She went down a spiralling set of stone steps and then he was reaching past her to push open another heavy door. A huge vast space with floor-to-ceiling glass windows was revealed as she stepped over the threshold.

'This is my apartment.'

Of *course* he had the apartment below the garden. Above the nightclub. He probably owned the building.

'Make yourself comfortable. How do you like your coffee?'

Rose was momentarily distracted by the views outside the massive windows. 'White with one sugar, please.'

She walked into the casual living space, with lots of luxurious-looking sofas and sleek coffee tables, strewn with big photography and art books. A media centre was set up on shelves that formed a dividing wall, with well-thumbed books and DVDs.

The stark minimalism of a quintessential bachelor pad was evident, but it was softened.

'Coffee?'

Rose jumped at his voice where she'd been standing, looking at his DVDs, and took the cup he held out, noticing that he'd taken off his jacket and waistcoat, so now he was just wearing the open-necked white shirt and trousers.

He gestured with his head towards the shelves. 'Don't tell anyone about my predilection for vintage Kung-Fu movies, will you?'

Rose forced a smile and tried to ignore the sensation of her heart turning over. 'I won't.'

The lights of the vast city around them lit up the huge space and it was impossibly seductive. She moved towards a window, cupping her hands around the mug in a bid to put some space between them.

Drink the coffee and get out—before you get lost again.

She marvelled at the life of privilege Zac enjoyed. Although he didn't give off the air of complacency and entitlement that she'd experienced from others. People like his parents...his mother. Her insides cramped.

'So...when you say you're a maid...?'

Zac's words scattered her guilt and Rose looked at him. She had to bite back a smile at his curious expression. She said dryly, 'It means that I'm one of those invisible workers who tidies up your world so that when you turn around nothing is out of place.'

He winced. 'Ouch.'

Rose shrugged. 'It's the way it is.'

'You don't sound bitter,' he observed.

She glanced at him again. She wasn't bitter at all. It had never bothered her that she came from a solidly working-class background. She'd had the love of two parents and knew that that was the most important thing in the world. Which was why she had to save her father...

Rose quickly averted her gaze from that incisive blue one. She felt sick and guilty again. She couldn't do this.

She put down her cup on a nearby table and straightened and looked at him, steeling herself. But her words dried in her mouth. Zac was looking at her with such searing explicitness that a shiver of anticipation raced through her.

She instructed herself with silent desperation. Say, *Thank you for the coffee, but I really should be going. Because I never would have met you in a million years if it hadn't been for—*

And then Zac said, 'Why do I think that you're about to bolt, and that if you do I'll never see you again?'

CHAPTER THREE

ZAC'S WORDS IMPACTED on Rose like a punch in the gut. *Because I am, and you won't.* She knew that if she walked out of there right now she wouldn't see him again, because this had been an exercise in madness.

She'd never in a million years expected to find herself in this situation, and maybe that was why she'd agreed to this extreme plan—because it had never entered her head that it could possibly become a reality.

Yet despite that she *was* there, and what had sprung to life between them was...unprecedented. It called to all of Rose's unawakened desires. And she knew that if she wanted—against all the odds—she might quite possibly be able to fulfil the demands of his mother.

But she couldn't do it.

Not now that she'd met him.

She couldn't deceive this man and use him in whatever power play was going on with his mother. She had no right. And she should never have been tempted. Jocelyn Lyndon-Holt had appealed to her fear and vulnerability. Her lack of resources. And she'd shamelessly taken advantage of Rose's father's ill health to do so.

For a moment Rose had been terrified enough to agree. But now, facing the stark reality of putting the plan into action, she knew she couldn't live with herself if she did.

She would have to find another way to try and save her father. Which was what she would have had to do anyway. If she walked out of here right now they would be no worse off than if she hadn't done this. She'd do anything but play with someone else's life.

She reiterated more firmly, 'I have to go.'

Bright blue eyes bored into hers and a hand closed around her upper arm. 'Why? Give me one good reason.'

Anger spiked in Rose—anger that she was in this predicament with the one man she couldn't have.

She pulled her arm free. 'Because I'm not meant to be here.'

'Says who?'

Rose glared at Zac and the anger bubbling up inside her was projected easily onto his arrogant tone.

She crossed her arms over her chest. 'Not *everyone* has to bow down to the mighty Zac Valenti.'

Zac's cheeks flushed with dull colour. 'I don't expect everyone to bow down to me.'

But they always will just because of who you are.

That wasn't fair. Rose's anger drained away. He was not the object of her ire. He was the object of something else—something much darker and hotter. And if she didn't get out now... Panic made her jerky as she looked around for her small clutch bag.

She couldn't see it, and she stopped and took a breath, looked back at Zac. 'I'm sorry. But I just...really have to go.'

Something in his expression hardened—again that glimpse of a more intimidating side. Intractability.

'You're married? You have a lover?'

Shocked, Rose answered with affront. '*No!* Nothing like that.'

Now he folded his arms across his chest. 'Then tell me,

Rose, why do you have to run?' He looked at his watch.
'Because it might be approaching midnight, but I don't
think you'll turn into a pumpkin when the clock strikes,
and you still have both your shoes.'

Something weakened inside Rose—some resistance
she was desperately clinging on to. Zac filled her vision,
filled every sense with his sheer charisma and masculine
allure. And all of it was fixated on her.

She heard herself admitting, 'I don't want to leave.'

His stern expression immediately relaxed. He uncrossed
his arms and stepped close to her again, cupping her jaw
with a hand. 'Then don't. Stay, sweet Rose. Stay with me
for tonight.'

She looked up into fathoms-deep, clear blue eyes and
fell headlong into a dream where she *did* stay, and spent
one beautiful, illicit night with the most exciting man she'd
ever met.

A seductive voice whispered over her feverishly hot
skin. *You can do this if you really want to...take this night
and keep it your secret forever.*

Just then a shrill sound pierced the thick silence. Rose
blinked out of the fantasy being woven in her head and
saw Zac's face tighten with irritation as he plucked a small
phone out of his pocket. He looked at the screen and is-
sued a curse.

He glanced at her. 'I'm sorry, I have to take this for a
moment...it's an important call I've been waiting for. But
don't move...'

The phone kept ringing—insistent. Zac was looking at
her, commanding her to his will, waiting for her promise
that she wouldn't leave.

Rose finally said, huskily, 'Okay...'

But as she watched him walk away from her, with that

powerful, lithe grace, she knew she'd just uttered a lie. This was her last chance. She had to leave—now.

At least, she told herself as she found her bag and stole out of the apartment, she wouldn't be adding any further transgressions to her already blackened soul. She wouldn't be betraying this man.

And she would never see him again.

Her chest grew tight and she bit her lip hard in the lift on her way back down to the ground level—a not so subtle reminder of where she belonged in the world. Not in the lofty heights of fantasy land, but here on the streets, among the millions of other anonymous New Yorkers who *never* got to taste the rarefied world inhabited by people like Zac Valenti.

Rose left through the main lobby and sent up silent thanks that George, the doorman, appeared to be busy with other residents. He barely spared her a glance.

When she emerged into the street she saw Zac's car and driver nearby and quickly took off in the other direction, hailing a cab. She knew what she had to do now.

When she returned to the Lyndon-Holt residence, she slipped in through the staff entrance and went straight to the staffroom, where she'd left her own clothes after dressing earlier.

When she'd changed, at the last minute she obeyed a rogue urge, packing up the beautiful sparkly dress, knowing that it was wrong. But it would be the only tangible reminder she would have of a beautiful night with a beautiful man when the possibilities had seemed endless—even if just for a moment.

She crept back out of the house, after leaving a note for Mrs Lyndon-Holt.

I'm sorry, the plan didn't work.
I'm resigning with immediate effect.

A short while later, on the subway back out to Queens, Rose swayed with the carriage and clutched her bag close on her lap, telling herself that it was ridiculous to feel such a sense of loss. She'd met Zac Valenti and been bathed in the sun of his incredible aura like thousands of other women—for a brief moment.

She was nothing special to him. She'd intrigued him, that was all, with her gauche manners and unsophistication. She was doing the right thing. The only thing she *could* do. She wanted her father to get better more than anything, but not at the expense of playing with someone else's life.

A week later Rose was walking home from doing some shopping with her fast-dwindling savings. Luckily she'd got a job working a few hours a week in a local health food store, but she would need other work—and fast—if she was to try and add to their health insurance so her father would be in with a shot to get on a waiting list for the operation he needed.

But that will take months, a small voice reminded her. *Months he doesn't have.*

Rose willed down the panic. She could do this. She was young, healthy. Relatively strong. She would work five jobs if she could find them.

She didn't regret walking away from her job in the Lyndon-Holt house. No way could she face that woman again. She felt tarnished even knowing what she'd agreed to, knowing what she'd almost done.

She was so engrossed in her thoughts that she barely noticed the sleek black car crawling beside her and coming to a stop at the same time as she did when she went to cross the road.

A prickling sensation stopped her in her tracks, though,

and she looked to see an all too familiar figure emerging from the back of the car, where the door was being held open by a driver.

As if conjured straight out of her thoughts by some nefarious alchemy, Mrs Lyndon-Holt stood resplendent in her designer clothes against the backdrop of the tired Queens street and said superciliously, 'Won't you join me in the car, Rose? I think we have some things to discuss.'

Hours later, dressed in a white shirt, black bow tie and knee-length black skirt, with her unruly hair in a neat bun on the top of her head, Rose held a tray of hors d'oeuvres aloft so that guests could help themselves.

Mrs Lyndon-Holt's cold voice still rang in her head. 'Do I need to remind you that you signed a legal document? I could sue you for breach of contract if you give up now.'

Rose had protested vociferously in the back of the car, to no avail. She'd even tried to convince the woman that Zac had asked her to leave.

The response to that had been, 'If Zachary isn't interested in you then why has he spent the week looking for you?'

Rose's heart had palpitated, and she'd asked shakily, 'How can you even know that?'

The other woman had waved a hand dismissively. 'I know everything my son is involved in. Believe me. And he wants you.'

Stupidly, Rose had given herself away by saying, 'He does?'

Mrs Lyndon-Holt had snapped impatiently, 'Of course he's interested, you stupid girl. By running away from him you've ensured his interest. Women do not evade Zachary Lyndon-Holt, and my son seems to have found your particular brand of unsophistication intriguing.'

As if Rose needed that reminder.

Her protests that she hadn't run away as part of an attempt to entice him had fallen on deaf ears. And Mrs Lyndon-Holt had reminded Rose cruelly of her other concerns when she'd said, 'Don't forget who you're doing this for, Rose. Your father. *He* doesn't deserve to suffer for your lack of action, does he?'

In the end, the not so subtle threat of legal action and a reminder of why she'd signed the contract in the first place had had Rose reluctantly accepting a note with an address on it and terse instructions from Mrs Lyndon-Holt as to what to wear.

So that was why she was now serving at a buffet luncheon inside one of Manhattan's most exclusive addresses, which housed one of the world's most famous private art collections, only on view to a very select few on occasions like this, once or twice a year.

Rose prayed that Zac wouldn't appear, and assured herself that even if he did he probably wouldn't even remember her, in spite of what his mother claimed.

But just as she was thinking that a very perceptible hush went around the room and she looked up to see him entering through the main salon door.

The tray nearly tipped out of her hands and she had to cling on for dear life. Her nerves went haywire and her blood sizzled. He was dressed in a dark grey three-piece suit and listening attentively to something the host was saying as he greeted him.

Rose couldn't breathe. She was suddenly filled with sheer dread that he would turn his head and see her.

On a panicky reflex, she swung around to try and stay out of his line of vision—and crashed straight into another server who was right behind her. Her tray was already unstable in her hands, and Rose watched helplessly as it collided with the other silver platter and they both tipped up and turned end over end, spraying horrified guests nearby with slivers of exotic hors d'oeuvre fillings before crashing to the undoubtedly priceless oriental carpet on the floor.

A deathly silence filled the air.

Zac was trying to appear interested in what the host was saying, but as per usual his mind was elsewhere. Specifically fixated on about five foot seven of *elsewhere*. A woman with slim curves and strawberry blonde hair. And the face of an angel that inspired distinctly *un*-angelic thoughts and desires.

He still couldn't believe she'd actually left that night. After looking at him with those wide green eyes and saying *okay*. He shouldn't have taken the call. She'd slipped through his fingers like shimmering quicksilver, impossible to hold onto.

No woman had walked away from Zac. *Ever.* And while that admittedly did add to the intrigue, the insatiable desire she'd roused inside him was unprecedented. And the need to know more about her. And why the hell hadn't his team found her yet?

Suddenly there was a loud metallic clatter, and Zac jerked his head around to see two trays spewing their contents and crashing to the floor. At the same moment that he was sending up silent thanks for being released from the attention of his host he was also noticing a very distinctive reddish blonde head of hair near the area of sudden carnage. Tucked up into a bun. Above a long neck.

His insides clenched—hard. It couldn't be her. But then she turned her head ever so slightly in his direction and he saw a familiar profile. Paler than pale skin...

It was her. Recognition washed over him in a dizzy-

ing sweep of heat and relief. Zac was not letting her slip
through his fingers again.

Rose had gone cold and clammy, all fingers and thumbs
as she tried to gather up the detritus of expensive cana-
pés. The other server hissed at her. 'What is *wrong* with
you? You've probably cost us both our jobs and I *need*
this work.'

Rose's gut lurched and she looked at the other girl's
blazingly angry expression. 'I'm so sorry. I don't know—'

'Now,' an assured and deep voice cut in, 'I don't think
anyone is going to lose their jobs over a simple accident—
are they, Mr Wakefield?'

Rose went still. *That voice.* Right above her head. *His*
voice. She looked to her left and saw expensively shod
feet.

Someone else was saying something brightly—'Not at
all. Please, let's just move aside and get this cleared up.'—
and then Rose felt a hand under her upper arm, curling
around it, and she was being urged upwards.

All the way up until she was standing in front of a familiar broad chest. She couldn't find enough breath to suck
into her lungs. She was barely aware of people cleaning
up and Zac leading her away from the site of the accident.
She was surprised her legs were working; she couldn't
feel them.

He was opening a door and urging her through, into a
dark-panelled room full of books. Rose felt as if she was
in a dream, and put it down to the fact that she was probably hyperventilating.

'Are you okay?'

She finally looked up and those blue eyes were even
brighter than she remembered. His jaw was clean-shaven.
She wanted to touch it. She expected he had to shave twice

a day to keep it like this. He'd had stubble that night of the ball—she could remember the slight burn on her skin after they'd kissed.

She nodded. 'You…you recognise me?'

Zac's mouth quirked. 'I met you a week ago, Rose. My memory still functions pretty well. And you were memorable—even if you did run.'

Thankfully the haze cleared from her head. She pulled her arm free and stepped back into the room.

Zac leaned against the door and put his hands in his pockets. As nonchalantly as if he owned the place.

'You said you'd stay.' He sounded accusing.

Rose was defensive. 'I didn't…exactly. I said, *okay*. But I knew I had to leave…'

'Why?'

Rose turned to avoid that incisive gaze. She felt as if she was being torn in two: torn between the part of her that was euphoric to see him again and the part of her that knew it was all a set-up.

She turned back to face him and gestured with a hand to her uniform and practical flat black shoes. 'Because this is who I am.' That, at least, was true. 'I'm not in your league, Mr Valenti, and I think you're only attracted to me because I'm a bit different.'

Zac straightened from the door, tension in his form. 'You're different, all right, and it's because you outshine any of those other women out there.'

Rose looked at him, helpless against his sheer power to suck her in again. 'Please, don't say that. It's not true.'

He prowled closer, and Rose backed away until she had to stop because there was a wall of books at her back. He crowded her, but she didn't feel threatened. She felt as if she was unfurling from the inside out. Like a flower blooming in the sun.

'I thought we'd moved on from Mr Valenti?'

He reached out and with deft fingers undid the bun on the top of her head. Her hair fell down around her shoulders. He sifted through it and Rose felt ridiculously like purring.

'I prefer it like this…a little wild and untamed.'

Her heart thudded against her breastbone.

Zac's blue eyes speared her to the spot then. 'You're a hard woman to find—do you know that?'

'You looked for me?' Rose hadn't really believed it, and to hear it confirmed, by him, was intoxicating.

He nodded. 'I couldn't get you out of my head or forget how you tasted…so sweet.'

Rose struggled not to let her legs turn to jelly and collapse under her. 'That's just because I left…you're not used to women walking away.'

Something flashed in those mesmerising eyes and his mouth became hard. 'I don't play games, Rose.'

It took her a second to register that he thought she was saying she'd left on purpose. She shook her head. 'I didn't leave just to be a tease. I left because I knew I had to…'

Just as you should leave now—before this goes too far. Again.

'Why fight this, Rose? The attraction between us is… combustible.'

Zac cupped her jaw with his hand and tipped her chin up. He put his other hand on her hip and lowered that beautiful face to hers. It was combustible, all right, and Rose couldn't make herself move out of the combustion zone.

His mouth settled on hers and it felt so right. So necessary. So exciting.

After a moment's hesitation Rose lifted her arms to wrap them around his neck. She wanted to arch her body into his and trembled with the effort it took not to do that. She felt Zac's hum of approval as he gathered her even closer. Her breasts were pressed against his chest, her nipples hardening at the contact.

A persistent knocking sound finally broke through the bubble encasing them. Zac pulled back, eyes hot, impatience stamped on his face. He called out, 'Yes?'

'Mr Valenti? Mr Wakefield is looking for you.'

Zac cursed quietly, but didn't take his eyes off Rose. 'Tell him I have to leave. Something came up. I'll call him.'

The disembodied voice floated through the door. 'Very well, sir.'

Zac looked at her for a long moment. 'I have never wanted a woman the way I want you, Rose.'

Something about the rawness of his tone got to her, and she bit her lip to stop herself from blurting out something similar. Then he took her hand and started to lead her over to another door in the room.

She tried to stop him. 'Wait—I'm working here. I have to go back outside.'

'Not any more. You're coming with me.'

Rose yanked her hand free, panic mixing with excitement at his autocratic tone. 'Now, wait just a minute. You can't make me lose my job.'

The fact that she had only been given the job for the day, thanks to whatever strings this man's mother had pulled, was forgotten in the face of his sheer arrogance.

His jaw hardened. 'You can go back out there and continue serving, with me hovering over your shoulder, or you can come with me now. And if the job is so damn important I can get you another job anywhere in this city by tomorrow morning.'

Rose just looked at him. Speechless.

He took advantage of it and came closer. 'I'm not letting you out of my sight again. So we can do this the quick way, by leaving now, or the slow way by leaving later. Up to you.'

Rose thought of proving the point by returning to work, but with Zac hovering at her heels she'd drop many more trays before her shift was over, and she'd already drawn enough attention to herself for one day.

As if he knew she was wavering he said, 'Stop overthinking it. This is simple. I want to get to know you.'

Rose had gone with him. Of course she had. Because she was weak and because she'd wanted to, as much as she feared the malevolence of Mrs Lyndon-Holt and what the future held for her father if she didn't comply.

She hadn't been sure what to expect once she'd agreed to leave with him, but Zac had asked his driver to stop in Central Park, and they'd walked through the park, hands linked. They'd talked about inconsequential things, like books, movies and their mutual love of the New York Yankees.

He'd bought them ice-cream from a vendor, and now they sat and looked across the Jacqueline Kennedy Onassis Reservoir as people jogged past.

Rose sneaked him a look, asked, 'Shouldn't you be working?'

He tipped his head up to the early-evening sun and closed his eyes, before opening them again and looking at her. He winked. 'I'm playing hooky.'

Rose's heart somersaulted in her chest. Never in a million years would she have imagined spending a couple of hours in Zac Valenti's company like this—as if he was just some regular guy and *not* one of America's most talked about billionaires. During the last week she'd seen the latest edition of *Forbes* magazine on the newsstands, with his picture on the front and the headline: *The most powerful new billionaire in America?*

Dusk was falling over Manhattan by the time they emerged on the south side of the park, and Rose could see Zac's building in the distance.

'I can see your garden from here.' She pointed up to where the green foliage peeked out over the walls.

When Zac didn't say anything she looked at him. His tie was undone, top button open. His jacket was hanging off a finger, draped over his shoulder casually. Hair ruffled by the breeze. Rose's heart squeezed tight. *Oh, boy.* She was in trouble.

He turned to face her. 'I can't believe I'm saying this, but there's a subway stop right across the street—or I could have my car take you home.'

For a moment Rose's belly plummeted. He didn't want her. Not after talking to her and realising how boring she was.

And then he continued, 'But I don't want you to go home. I want you to come with me and spend the night with me.'

She reeled at his stark words as illicit relief rushed through her body. Take it or leave it. No games. He wanted her, and he wasn't going to waste time pretending otherwise. She wished right then that she wasn't in such a bind, that she could freely accept what Zac was offering with no strings attached. But every which way she moved now the strings were getting tighter and tighter.

She was still deceiving him. With every breath she took.

She pulled her hand free of his and stepped back unsteadily, as if drunk from his mere presence all over again.

She shook her head, feeling a rush of burning emotion. 'I'm sorry... I just *can't*.'

Right now she would prefer to risk Mrs Lyndon-Holt's wrath than betray this man. She took another step, and another. She looked across the road and took advantage of a lull in the traffic to run across.

Heart thudding painfully, she stopped on the other side and looked back at Zac. He cut a powerful and proud figure. Face hard. He wouldn't chase her again. She knew it. She'd intrigued him for a brief moment—*again*—but a man like him would soon forget about a maid who kept playing hard to get. And his mother would find someone else to deceive him.

She had to focus on her father—not complicate their lives by potentially becoming pregnant on purpose!

Rose knew there would be no shortage of women who would go all the way with this plan without feeling her angst-ridden turmoil. And suddenly she was angry at that thought—which was ironic, considering that she was the one currently deceiving him!

This was so messed up. She had to go.

She walked with heavy feet to the subway entrance and looked down into the cavernous dark opening. It was dark and cold and dank. She was jostled by rush hour crowds, eager to get home.

She looked across the road again and Zac was still standing there. Vital and bathed in sunlight. Rose had never wanted anything so much as to walk back across to him. She wanted to forget her responsibilities. She wanted to forget the strings. She wanted to pretend that she'd met him by coincidence, exactly as he believed.

She didn't want to go down into that cold dark hole and never see Zac again.

The fantasy she'd woven in her head for a brief moment

that night, when she'd admitted to him she didn't want to go, just before his phone had rung, beckoned again like a siren call...

You can do this if you want...take what he's offering and walk away.

She wavered. Could she...really?

Rose knew she couldn't tell him everything, but what if she was brutally honest about how innocent she was? Surely she'd lose her appeal then? A man used to experienced lovers, he'd hardly relish teaching a novice...

And if he still wanted her even then—her heart beat fast at that prospect—she'd make sure that there would be no pregnancy. *He* would make sure. After all, wasn't that exactly what those women in the powder room of that hotel had said? Zac Valenti was the last man to allow himself to be caught in such a way.

Rose turned against the tide of people rushing around her. As if sensing her capitulation from across the road Zac came towards her, like a panther intent on his prey. His eyes were locked onto hers until he was standing in front of her.

A silent communication passed between them. *Are you sure? No more games.*

And from the deepest part of her came just one word as she put her hand in his: *Yes.*

Zac felt euphoric. He felt reckless. Out of his comfort zone. As if he was going slightly crazy.

Since when had he ever taken a notion to walk across Central Park in the afternoon, to hold a woman's hand? Or to stop and buy ice-cream? Or to take time out from work. Something he hadn't done in...*ever.*

But from the moment he'd seen Rose again in that room his brain had ceased functioning normally.

The only thing stopping him from slamming a hand on the *'Stop'* button of his private elevator right now and lifting her against the wall with her legs wrapped around his waist, so he could take her right here, was the tiniest sliver of control that reminded him he was a civilised man and not an animal.

It was the only thing that had held him back from cursing when she'd pulled away and crossed the road just a short while before. But then she'd stood at the entrance of that subway, looking into it as if it held some answer...and she hadn't moved. And she'd looked across at him and her hunger and yearning had been palpable.

He'd wanted to howl in triumph. Because he'd known then that this mysterious, fey woman who had bewitched his body and mind was going to be *his*. He would get her mysterious pull out of his system and put it behind him.

This last week had shown him that he was more at the mercy of his hormones than he'd like to admit. For a man who had always felt in control of his life—even when it had spun in a completely unexpected direction—it was a disturbing sensation. He didn't equate women with hormones or this craving need.

He came from a world where logic ruled. Where emotions showed up weaknesses. From a young age, his life was lived by a strict code of rules. Even if he thought he'd thrown all that out of the window, he hadn't really. He just lived by a different set of rules now.

If anything had demonstrated to him that emotions out of control spelled doom, his own parents' legacy had. Their lives—and his—had been ruined by reckless passion. And while he wanted to avenge them above anything else, he also wanted to prove that he could control himself. That his life wouldn't be derailed as theirs had been.

Rose held him momentarily in thrall, and he didn't like it. He didn't trust it. So the sooner he could exorcise it, the better. And this was just the start.

CHAPTER FOUR

ZAC'S APARTMENT WAS subtly different from the other night as the setting sun bathed it in a golden light. Rose was breathing too rapidly and forced herself to slow down. She'd taken her hand out of Zac's when they'd come into the apartment and walked over to one of the windows, suddenly jittery. Suddenly wondering again if she was being completely crazy—not to mention selfish.

She looked out and put a hand on the glass, as if that might help to anchor her in this fantastical space. He came to stand beside her and the air quivered between them. That damned breathlessness was back, along with a spurt of panic.

What was she doing here?

She gabbled words to try and fill the weighted silence. 'It's so beautiful up here. You're very lucky.'

Zac's voice was deep and low beside her. 'I know how beautiful it is and, believe me, I know how lucky I am.'

She finally looked at him and he was leaning with his back against the glass, which suddenly looked totally flimsy to Rose. He'd removed his tie and taken off his waistcoat, and was staring at her assessingly.

She felt acutely self-conscious. She wore only a minimum amount of make-up, which had probably melted off by now, making her face shiny. Her hair was down and messy, thanks to him. She wore the blandest of clothes. As opposite as she could be from the woman he'd met a week ago.

Unbidden, she asked helplessly, 'Why do you want me?'

His eyes rose from where they'd been making a lazy appraisal of her body and met hers, piercingly blue. 'Because you're more beautiful than anything I've ever seen in my life.'

'I'm not—really I'm not...' Rose ducked her head and her hair slipped forward, covering her face.

Zac pushed it back behind one ear and tipped her face up with a finger under her chin. She couldn't look anywhere but at him. He was standing in front of her now.

'Yes, you are, Rose. And I want you because of that and also because I won't be able to think again until I have you.'

She could feel herself slipping down a rabbit hole, with nothing to grab on to at the sides. Except for Zac.

He moved closer and closer, until their bodies were touching and she was drowning in his scent. She grabbed his shirt in order to stay standing, trying not to fall down the hole completely. And then he lowered his head and her world was reduced to this: *yes*.

His kisses were like nectar—but with a darkness that called to some alien dark part of her. That was why she was really there. She was weak and she wanted to taste the forbidden too much.

She moaned with a kind of angry self-despair into Zac's mouth and he clearly took that as encouragement, sliding his tongue deep, dancing and duelling with hers. The kiss turned deeper and more lustful.

Zac's hand dropped to her waist, and then further. He squeezed one buttock through the material of her skirt, his hand easily encompassing the firm flesh.

Rose ripped her mouth away, unable to think how to do more than one thing at once any more. She rested her forehead against his neck, breathing rapidly. Zac moved back slightly, but only so he could bring her over to a nearby couch. He sat down and on jelly legs Rose followed him, falling into his arms, sprawling across his lap.

She tried to sit up but he wouldn't let her, saying, 'I like you like this.'

Rose just looked at him, and he kissed her again, and she forgot to protest. He was smoothing a hand down over her chest, cupping a breast, squeezing gently. She gasped into his mouth.

And then his hand was untucking her shirt from her skirt so he could explore underneath, touching her skin, moving higher, cupping her breast again more intimately, finding her nipple under its lace covering and pinching it gently.

Rose tore her mouth from his again and looked at him, feeling feverish. Zac pulled down the lace of her bra and now his hand was on her bared breast. He looked feral, hungry.

'Undo the buttons of your shirt. I want to see you.'

With shaking hands she did his bidding, like some kind of wanton robot. Her shirt fell open and Zac looked down. Colour scored his cheeks.

He muttered, 'Just how I imagined…beautiful.' And then he lowered his head and kissed her breast, tasting the hard bud of her nipple, licking the pouting flesh and sucking it into his mouth like a succulent morsel.

Zac bared her other breast and anointed that one with his hot mouth and rough tongue. She had to press her thighs together to try and contain the building tension deep in her core.

But, like a mind-reader, Zac was sliding his hand between her thighs now, forcing her to part them for him. She looked at him again, aware that her shirt was wide open, her breasts bared and upthrust, framed by her bra.

He pressed against her sex through her underwear. Fingers exploring, sliding up and down. One of Rose's hands gripped his arm, as if that might keep her anchored. She couldn't believe she was behaving so wantonly, letting him touch her so intimately, urging her to fall over a precipice that she'd only explored by herself before now.

But she couldn't find a voice to tell him to stop.

Zac pushed the gusset of her underwear aside and then he was touching her with expert precision, knowing exactly *where* she ached. Rose bit her lip. He kept looking at her as his fingers slipped through her slick folds, unlocking all her secrets, and then dipped inside her…gently at first and then with increasing pressure as he forged a deeper and deeper passage, rhythmically, remorselessly.

His thumb massaged her clitoris, and Rose tried valiantly to cling on to control of her own body, but it was impossible. She came apart in his arms, head thrown back as all her muscles locked tight. She could feel herself clenching and shuddering, completely defenceless against such a rush of pleasure.

It seemed to take an aeon for her to come back to earth, floating on a cloud of satisfaction she'd never experienced before. She lifted her heavy head, feeling dazed.

Zac was still looking at her, and he said with a touch of sensual approval, 'You're so *responsive*.'

And then Rose saw herself as he did—bared from the waist up and from the waist down. Legs spread. She went hot all over—hot with mortification. They'd been in the apartment for mere minutes and she was already writhing and moaning on his lap—a million miles from the sophisticated responses he was undoubtedly used to.

She scrambled free of his embrace and moved to the end of the couch, tugging her skirt down and pulling her shirt back together. She knew her legs wouldn't hold her up without shaking.

Zac sat up. 'Rose...what is it?'

She didn't hear him. She was berating herself. She should have told him the truth before now. Hadn't that been part of the bargain she'd made to herself to justify coming here with him? But she'd forgotten in the heat of the moment. She was meant to be trying to put him off—not lead him on.

'Rose?'

Her whirling thoughts came to an abrupt halt and she looked at Zac, who was beside her now. Stubble was already marking his jawline. His hair flopped forward and the strong lines of his face were breathtakingly distracting, even now.

'There's something you need to know,' she said in a husky voice. 'I'm a virgin.'

Zac struggled to understand through the fog of lust clouding his brain. 'What did you say?'

Her cheeks coloured dark red, and she said it again—starkly. 'I'm a virgin.'

For the longest moment he could only look at her. She might as well have said that there was a unicorn on the other side of the room—that was how little he could understand what she was saying. Then her words slowly impacted and he thought of how responsive she'd just been, and he noticed how she was holding her clothes together...

He suddenly needed space. He stood up and asked a little hoarsely, 'How old are you?'

'Twenty-two.'

Zac shook his head, as if it might encourage his brain cells to start working properly again. 'And you've never…?'

Rose stood now too, arms crossed over her shirt to try and hold it together. Her skirt was still ruched up over her thighs. She looked dishevelled…undone. Sexy as hell. And he could see that she didn't have a clue how alluring she was.

Something inside him tightened.

She avoided his eyes. 'I've never had a boyfriend—not like that. I never wanted to have sex with anyone… It's just me and my father at home. He found it hard to cope after my mother died, so I never went out much…'

The tightening sensation in his chest increased and Zac reeled as this revelation of her innocence sank in fully. It struck him powerfully—especially after all the secrets and lies he'd found in his own family. The tragedy that had ensued as a result of them.

He knew he should be sending her away. He didn't *do* virgins. Just as he didn't do relationships. He was from a world that had stripped away any illusion that innocence or happy families existed a long time ago… And yet he found that he couldn't make himself do what he knew he should.

He moved closer to Rose and reached out and put a finger under her chin, tipping her face up. As soon as their gazes met he knew that he was not letting her go. In spite of her innocence. He wanted to claim her for himself with a fierceness that shook him.

'You said you've never wanted to have sex with anyone…do you now?'

After a long moment that had all Zac's nerves stretched taut enough to snap, Rose nodded.

Honesty was something he prized now, above almost anything else, and right at that moment this woman in front of him stood for something he'd never experienced before. A kind of purity.

He closed the gap between them and pulled her closer, his thumb sliding across skin as soft as a rose petal. She'd been named well.

She looked at him, something swirling in those big green eyes. 'You're not...sending me away?'

The thought made Zac feel feral. He hid it. 'Why would I do that?'

She swallowed. 'Because I'm not experienced.'

Her expression of bravado mixed with something much more vulnerable made him feel inordinately protective. He shook his head. 'No way, sweet Rose. You're not going anywhere.'

Her eyes flared at that. She was hungry for him. And he was ravenous—even more so now.

He reached for her hand to lead her into his bedroom before he took her on the floor like an animal, but she squeezed his hand and he stopped to look at her. She was pale now...worried.

'I'm not...on the pill. You need to protect us.'

Relief made Zac's chest expand. For a moment he'd been afraid she'd changed her mind. But she was concerned about protection. And so was he. Zealously so. This should be the least of her worries.

He slid a hand around to the back of her head, under her hair, and pressed his mouth to hers. Already his body was responding with a carnal hunger that he knew wouldn't wait.

He pulled back. 'Don't worry, I'll make sure we're protected—believe me.'

Her concern only made her honesty even more pronounced. Zac knew well that if she was more experienced she might see the knots he was tied in and take advantage of that. But she wasn't.

He led her into his bedroom, anticipation coiling in his gut like a living thing. There was something incredibly raw and visceral about knowing that no other man had touched this woman. That he would be the first to mark her...brand her. She would be indelibly *his*.

He shook his head faintly, as if to try and dislodge these uncharacteristically primal flights of fancy. He associated animalistic feelings with the boardroom. Not the bedroom. Or he had up till now.

He let Rose's hand go and turned to face her at the foot of his bed. Her eyes were huge. Her mouth was still swollen from his kisses. The hard tips of her breasts were evident under the material of her shirt.

He had to exert control. She was innocent. He was almost afraid to touch her. Not sure if he could control himself. He uttered a silent curse. He'd never felt on edge like this before.

'Take off my shirt.'

When she moved forward her own shirt opened more, and the tantalising curves of her bare breasts were visible through the open material.

He had to curl his hands into fists to stop himself from reaching out. And then she was grappling with his buttons, painstakingly slowly, undoing them one by one. Her fingers brushed against his hot skin in tantalisingly fleeting caresses.

Zac gritted his jaw. When he saw the tip of her tongue dart out, and the way she bit her lower lip in concentration, a bead of sweat broke out on his forehead. Her small hands were near his belt now, and he couldn't stand it any more. He took her hands in his and lifted them up, pressing a kiss to the centre of each palm.

Something in his chest squeezed tight again when he felt the slight roughness that told of her menial work. He felt incensed that she should have to do this, and hated himself in that moment for having always been with women who spent more money on their manicures than Rose probably saw in a year.

He dropped her hands and let them go, then yanked his shirt out of his trousers, pulling it off and letting it drop to the ground.

Her eyes were on his chest, wide and intent. Her cheeks flushed with colour. He could see her clench one hand into a fist, as if to stop herself from touching him, and he reached for it and brought it up, uncurling her fingers and placing it in the centre of his chest.

Her touch was cool, but it burned hotter than the most seductive caress. She looked up at him and he took his hand away, and hesitantly she started to explore. Tracing the muscles under his skin. When her nail scraped a nipple he sucked in a breath and his erection jerked in his pants. He'd never known how sensitive he was there.

'Did I hurt you?'

He shook his head and marvelled at the genuinely concerned look on her face. 'No—the opposite.'

The flush on her face deepened. Her hands were drifting down now, over his abdomen and lower. She was going to kill him. She reached for his belt and looked up, as if asking for permission.

He just nodded. Rendered speechless.

She undid it and then opened the button above the zip. Zac felt almost embarrassed at the prominent bulge in his pants.

Rose's head was down, her bright hair falling forward. Wilder than the other night, it was the most unusual colour. Blonde but with russet tones. He wondered if the unusual colour was natural. He would know for sure when he saw—

He stifled a gasp of pure pleasure/pain. She was lowering his zip now, her knuckles brushing against the swell of his arousal.

She looked up again and he gently took her hands away, muttering, 'I won't last if you keep touching me like that.'

'I'm sorry.'

Zac shook his head and cupped her jaw, tipping her face up. How could she not know what she was doing to him? *Because she was innocent.*

He grimaced slightly. 'Don't be.'

He let her go again to pull down his trousers, letting them drop to the floor. He stepped out of them and said, 'I want to see you.'

She bit her lip again for a moment and then brought her hands to her shirt, peeling it off slowly until it fell to the ground. Her breasts were still bared, and erotically upthrust by the underwired frame of her bra. Zac marvelled that he'd seen far more debauched states of undress on women, but this was possibly the most sensual thing he'd ever experienced.

She brought her hands behind her and undid her bra, and it too fell to the ground. Her high, perfectly formed breasts were now bared completely to his ravenous gaze. A small, hard, pink nipple topped each one. The darker pink of her areolae was puckered. His mouth watered. He wanted to taste them again.

She brought her arms up to cover herself. Gently he pulled them down.

'You are beautiful.'

'No one's ever seen me like this before.'

Blood thrummed in Zac's body at this further confirmation that he was the first man who would know her intimately. He ignored the tiny dim cynical voice that mocked him for being so easily entranced. He was losing it.

'Thank you for trusting me.'

Something flashed in her eyes then, but it was gone so quickly he thought he must have imagined it. Because it had almost looked like guilt. And why would she be guilty?

Rose undid her skirt and pushed it over her hips, and then she was standing in front of him in nothing but sensible white underwear—which, again, seemed to Zac to be the height of eroticism after years of seeing women parade in front of him in all sorts of complicated diaphanous concoctions.

Words and thoughts fused into white heat. She was all long, slim limbs and pale skin. Delicate curves. High waist. Freckles dusting her upper arms and her chest.

Curbing the beast inside him, Zac took her hand and led her over to the bed. 'Lie down, sweetheart.' The endearment tripped easily off his tongue, when he was usually much more circumspect. But he hardly noticed.

She sat on the bed and scooted back, her breasts bouncing with her movement. Zac yanked down his underwear and kicked it off, watching how Rose stopped, her eyes fixated on him. He brought a hand to himself, as if that might calm the heat a little, but her eyes widened and he could feel a drop of moisture dewing the head of his erection.

He reached for the protection he kept in a drawer nearby. He'd never had to have it ready like this before. Almost as if he might forget. Rose tracked his movements as she sat on her hands on the bed, legs tightly together, drawn up.

'Lie back.'

Slowly she lay down, eyes still on him, hair around her head like a cloud of red-gold. He came down alongside her on the massive bed, very aware of how dark his skin was next to hers.

He put a hand on her belly, stretched it out, almost encompassing all of it with the span. Her muscles jerked against him.

'I'm going to make this good for you…but it might hurt a little at first. Just trust me, okay?'

She nodded jerkily. He dipped his head and kissed her, long and luxuriously, drawing her as close to his body as he could without exploding. She was soft and silky, but quivering like a taut bow under his touch.

She gave herself to him with sweetly innocent abandon, but then suddenly drew back, going tense. She looked over his shoulder at the huge windows in his room. 'Won't people be able to see in?'

Zac recalled how one of his previous lovers had specifically wanted him to make love to her up against the glass, for that very reason. It left a bitter taste in his mouth now.

'No, it's specially tinted glass…'

'Oh…okay.'

She relaxed against him again and Zac smoothed a hand down from her neck to her breast, cupping it and squeezing the firm flesh, seeing how her nipple protruded like a sharp berry. Her breathing quickened—an untutored and totally sexy response. Zac prided himself on being a good lover, but right now he felt as if everything he knew was unravelling.

He bent and put his mouth to Rose's sweet offering, lights exploding behind his eyes as he ran his tongue over her tight flesh and then sucked it into his mouth. He could feast on her breasts for days, he thought, his erection growing even harder at the sounds of her soft, breathy moans and the way her hands found his head and her fingers tightened in his hair.

He slid the hand on her belly down to where her legs were pressed tight together. Gently he encouraged her to relax them, and she opened up. The musky smell of her arousal hit his nostrils and he had to lift his head for a second to clear it.

Her hands were still in his hair and she was looking up at him, flushed and dazed, green eyes huge. Mouth plump and pink. The tips of her breasts wet from his mouth.

His penis twitched at her look and he knew he couldn't hold on for much longer. He explored through the soft curls that hid the seam of her body and he almost groaned aloud when he felt how plumped and wet she was. Ready for him again.

He looked down as he efficiently pulled off her underwear. Soft golden curls hid her sex, and he couldn't resist the temptation to taste her. He moved down the bed and hooked her legs over his shoulders.

She lifted her head, eyes wide. 'Zac…?'

He just said, 'Shh, lie back.'

She did, and he pressed kisses to her soft inner thighs before exploring her more intimately. Her smell was more intoxicating than the most expensive perfume in the world. He licked his way through her secret folds and thrust his tongue into that tight channel.

Her hands were on his head, fingers digging in painfully, but not even that could distract him. He was getting drunk on her, flicking her clitoris, then thrusting deep again, fighting the urge to grind his hips to the bed and find his own relief.

She was pushing her body at him now and he reached up a hand to cup her breast, squeezing it hard just as she came—her body convulsing as powerfully as it had before.

A fractured thought occurred to him that he could never lose his hunger for this woman and her swift responses, but it was drowned out by his need to bury himself inside her or go mad.

He reared up to see a dreamy smile on her face. Perspiration sheened her skin, making it even more luminous.

Sheathing himself with the protection, Zac positioned himself between her legs. 'Ready?' He sounded coarse, guttural. Desperate.

She nodded, still looking a little drugged. He slid in carefully, just the head breaching her body first. She was still slick, but tight.

Her hands came to his arms, holding tight. 'I'm okay… keep going.'

Zac reached under her body and shifted her slightly, coming up on his knees, widening her thighs even further. She gasped as he slid in a little morc. He wrapped her legs around his hips.

He bent over her and put his mouth on hers, sucking her tongue deep, and then he thrust again…hard. He swallowed her gasp and met it with a rough gasp of his own. He was embedded deep in her hot, tight embrace.

He drew back. She was panting, nails digging into his muscles. His insides curdled when he saw how pale she was. 'Are you okay?'

She took a minute and then nodded. 'I…I think so.'

Zac reached down between them and found her sensitised bud. He massaged her gently, feeling a quiver of reaction along his length. He gritted his jaw, trying to stay in control of his bodily functions when all he wanted to do was pull out and thrust back in so hard and deep he'd see stars for a week.

He moved slowly, inexorably, out and then in again, feeling Rose's body relax its tighter-than-tight grip. Testosterone flooded him at the thought that he was the first man to experience this with her.

His arms wrapped tight around her as his powerful body struck up a rhythm, moving in and out. Any last vestiges of control were fast fraying at the edges as Rose's body responded, her legs squeezing tighter around him. Her nipples scraped against his chest.

And then, when her hips started to circle in small movements, he couldn't hold on. He thrust deep and long inside her, and somehow—miraculously—felt the telltale contractions of her own climax squeezing him just before he tipped over into a place of extreme pleasure so intense that he was aware of nothing for long moments but the frantic beating of his heart.

When he finally floated back to earth he realised he was crushing Rose into the bed, his body heavy on hers. His head was locked into the space between her neck and shoulder. Little weak pulsations rippled along his length every few seconds. His body responded. He raised his head to look down incredulously. Sex had *never* had this effect on him before.

Rose's head was turned to the side; her eyes were closed. She was no longer holding his arms and something cold gripped him, dousing his desire. He pulled free of her body and saw her wince slightly.

He'd felt her body react—he'd been sure she'd been okay... But had he taken his pleasure with no regard for her well-being? He moved down beside her and saw her legs close together—saw also the telltale sign of blood on his sheets. He felt as if someone had just punched him in the gut.

He pulled up a sheet, covering her body. His voice sounded unbearably rough to his ears. 'Rose...are you okay? Did I hurt you?'

Rose knew she couldn't avoid Zac's question forever. She could feel the weight of his gaze almost as tangibly as she'd felt the weight of his body. Deliciously. Surrounding her with his musky heat and hard muscles. Until a few moments ago he'd been inside her, a heavy thick weight. Still hard.

Slowly she turned to face him and saw his eyes widen with shock as he reared back.

'You're crying. I hurt you—but I thought—'

She hadn't even realised till then that she was crying, but she shook her head and wiped at a tear, feeling raw and exposed. 'No...' When she saw the blatant disbelief on his face and the start of something like self-recrimination, she came up on one arm, the sheet slipping down. '*No*. You *didn't* hurt me.' Her voice felt rough. Different.

He shook his head. 'Then...?'

Rose had never been so comprehensively laid bare, so she said honestly, 'I never knew it could be like that. It was...beautiful.'

She winced inwardly. 'Beautiful' was an ineffectual word for what had just happened. It had been brutal, searing...pain and pleasure all bound up in pure sensation and incandescence. And pleasure like she'd never known. Too much, surely?

Zac reached out and touched her jaw as if she might break. 'Are you sure?'

She nodded, turning her face into his hand, breathing him in deep. She looked back. 'At first...when you...' She blushed, stupidly. 'It hurt. But it didn't last...it became something else.'

Zac came down on his back and pulled Rose with him so she half fell across his chest, hair tumbling around her shoulders, breasts pressed against him. She thought of his mouth between her legs and blushed all over again.

He touched her burning cheek and half smiled, 'What are you thinking of?'

She ducked her head, embarrassed by how hungry she

was for him again—already. In spite of tender muscles.
'Nothing.'

'Liar,' he said. and she could hear the smile in his voice.

Her gut curdled. The truth was that this whole evening
was a lie. *But at least he used protection*, she thought with
relief, recalling all too easily how those big hands had
deftly rolled the latex over his impressive erection.

And then Zac was pressing her closer and saying, 'Rest
now.'

She knew that this was it—her time was up and she
should leave—but her body was so full and heavy with a
delicious afterglow that she just…clung to the dream for
a little longer and slept.

CHAPTER FIVE

WHEN ZAC WOKE up his body felt uncharacteristically heavy, and yet lighter than it had ever felt. He frowned, his eyes still closed. It was such an unusual sensation. He was aware that his penis also felt heavy, yet sated. His whole body ached in a way he'd never experienced before.

A vague thought occurred to him: *was he sick?*

And then a very distinctive feminine scent caught at his nostrils and he was suddenly wide awake. He opened his eyes. He wasn't sick. *Rose.* Sweet Rose...opening up to him with such abandon. And just like that his body was no longer heavy—it was waking up. Stirring.

A kaleidoscope of images crashed through his brain— firm breasts topped by small sharp nipples, pale slim thighs parting for him. His tongue tasting her sweet essence, feeling her muscles tighten around him, rose-gold hair, green eyes... Sliding into tight, slick heat...so tight he'd thought he might die.

Virgin. His.

He lifted his head and looked around his room, aware of the morning sun streaming in the windows. He never normally slept much beyond dawn, so this was disconcerting.

The bed beside him was empty, but the sheets were crumpled and her scent lingered. He hadn't dreamed it. But then, disconcertingly, slivers of a dream came back to him: her bottom tucked into the cradle of his body, her turning, lifting her face, angling herself so that he slipped between her legs...

He'd notched himself inside her, hearing her gasp... There were snippets and fragments of hushed whispers... *'Are you too sore?'*

She'd shaken her head, eyes glittering green. *'No, keep going...'*

And so Zac had, thrusting harder and deeper, one hand clamped around her breast, his other hand finding the juncture between her legs, close to where he surged in and out, touching her there and coming apart as she'd milked him so powerfully he'd stopped breathing...

Zac frowned. He hadn't used protection in the dream, and he would *never* not use protection, so it couldn't have been real. Even so, the back of his neck prickled... It felt as if it had been real.

And where was she now? He got up and pulled on some old sweats and went through his apartment after checking the bathroom. There was no sign of the woman who had spent the night in his bed. Or any indication that she'd used the bathroom.

The thought of her somewhere...with his scent on her body and the markings of their lovemaking on her pale skin...was enough to make his body go hard in an instant. Zac scowled. Where the hell *was* she?

But the apartment was empty. Silent. She was gone. *Again.* He felt deflated. A novel sensation for a man who usually left women in his wake. That prickling sensation was back. His apartment looked untouched... *Hell*, was he so desperate for a connection that felt real that he'd dreamt it all up? Had some crazy erotic fantasy?

But his gut told him that it had been real. His body was too heavy with sensual satisfaction for it to have been a mere erotic dream. Still…he doubted himself. He padded back through to the bedroom, not even sure what he was looking for until he saw it: the unmistakable mark of her blood on his sheets.

So it had been real. *She* was real.

He turned to face his windows. He didn't like it that she kept running away. It made him feel off-balance, exposed somehow…as if she knew something he didn't. As if he'd been caught out.

Zac looked out over the city, glinting in the early-morning sunlight. She was out there somewhere. He would find her… He would be successful this time. And then he would see that she was not some ethereal, mysterious creature who'd scrambled his brain to pieces—twice. And he would get her out of his system, like every other woman he slept with.

Because women like Rose Murphy didn't really exist. They just didn't.

In spite of Zac's best efforts he *didn't* find her. Not a week after she'd left, or a month, nor two months. It had now been four months since he'd had her in his bed and his body still burned for her. Only her. All other women left him cold.

It was exposing, infuriating and it reminded him uncomfortably of the repercussions of the passion that had burnt between his parents, which had ultimately led to their destruction and a life of secrets and lies for him, growing up in a gilded prison with two severe and unloving caretakers.

A knock sounded on his office door, and he turned from where he was looking out over the downtown Manhattan view with a brooding glower. 'Yes?'

His executive assistant came in, looking grim. 'We've got her, Zac. But I don't think you're going to like it.'

The feelings jostling for space in Zac's chest were nearly overpowered by the surge of heat in his blood. And then he frowned. 'What do you mean, I'm not going to like it?'

The younger man put one of New York's most popular newspapers down on Zac's desk, face up. A screaming headline proclaimed: *Real-life Maid in Manhattan scores the Lyndon-Holt jackpot with pregnancy!*

And underneath the headline was a picture of Rose... O'Malley, *not* Murphy...looking wild-eyed and hunted. Hair scraped back.

He assessed the situation in an instant as an icy weight slammed into his gut. One word exploded in his head: *Fool. Fool. Fool.*

He was right to have believed women like her didn't exist—because clearly they didn't. He skim-read the article, taking in the fact that she'd worked for his grandmother as a maid in his family home. Something dark lodged in his gut. He should have recognised his grandmother's handiwork. She had not been without the help of a willing accomplice, though...

The darkness spread like a seeping poison into the blood in his veins. He didn't look up from the paper. He was afraid to move in case he exploded into pieces. He just said, with a quiet, controlled tone that belied his growing rage, 'Find her and bring her to me. *Now.*'

Rose sat in the back of the chauffeur-driven car as they crossed the bridge onto the island of Manhattan. It wasn't as if she'd had a choice when that scarily taciturn man had turned up at her place of work and said, 'I'm here to take you to Mr Valenti.'

She'd known that this meeting was inevitable. She

guessed she'd known it as soon as she'd had the confirmation of her pregnancy about two months ago.

And, if she was completely honest with herself, she'd known far sooner than that—because they'd made love again that night, in the half-light of the moon, in the hazy, dreamlike moments between sleeping and waking.

Rose might have believed it to have been a dream if it hadn't been for the indelible memory of the pulsing strength of Zac's climax inside her. When she'd woken again as dawn had been breaking, she'd weakly tried to convince herself that it *had* just been a dream.

But it hadn't.

And, as terrified as she'd been to contemplate the fact that the night *would* have repercussions, she'd also felt an immediately fierce sense of acceptance and protectiveness for her unborn child—even before she'd missed her first period and her fears had become real.

Still, it had taken all of her guts and courage to go and have the pregnancy confirmed, because she'd had a very strong sense of foreboding that as soon as someone else knew about it she would be putting her child in some kind of perilous danger.

At no point—even when the pregnancy had been confirmed—had it occurred to her to go and tell Mrs Lyndon-Holt. Her only thought had been how she would eventually tell Zac. The fact that she now possibly had a way to save her father was something she hadn't allowed herself to contemplate, because she had known she wouldn't be able to live with herself if she used her unborn child as some kind of bargaining chip…and her father would never want his own flesh and blood used in that way either.

It had brought home to her just how distraught she'd

been even to consider that this might be a solution to her problems in the first place.

But she hadn't had to worry about going to see Mrs Lyndon-Holt because the woman had ambushed Rose. Just as she had before, and just when Rose had finally felt she was off the woman's radar after not seeing her in months.

Far from not being on the woman's radar, Rose discovered she had been very much on it. She hadn't figured on the ruthlessness of the woman, or her vast influence. And now everything had been taken out of her hands in the worst way possible.

In the back of that same sleek black limousine, parked on a quiet Queens street, Mrs Lyndon-Holt had swiped through photo after photo on a sleek tablet. The pictures had documented Rose and Zac leaving that luncheon function and walking through Central Park. They had shown the moments by the subway, when Rose had obviously made her fateful decision to stay. And then they'd shown her leaving his apartment the following morning as dawn had broken, looking dishevelled and with a mortifyingly dreamy and wistful look on her face. Wistful because she'd believed she'd never see him again.

There was no need for any photos of what had happened in the intervening hours. It was glaringly obvious.

And since then her every move had been followed. Mrs Lyndon-Holt had merely waited until Rose had passed the danger zone of early pregnancy before pouncing.

When Rose had tried to get out of the car the woman had restrained her with a brittle but surprisingly strong hand. Rose had looked back at her, feeling numb all over.

'Are you forgetting so easily about your payment?'

Rose had answered with a coolness that had belied the fear she'd felt, 'I don't want anything from you.'

The other woman had just smiled malevolently. 'Perhaps not you or the baby right now—but your father could do with some help, couldn't he? Or are you just going to let him die, knowing that you could have saved him if it wasn't for your stubborn pride? Do I need to remind you that you signed a non-disclosure agreement? Which means you can never tell anyone about what we agreed? And don't for a second think that my son will welcome this news. It's common knowledge that he has no desire for a child. So you see, Rose, I'm really all the hope and support you have right now. All I have to do is make one call and your father will have a chance to live to be a very old man.'

Rose had gone hot and then cold all over. As if she needed to be reminded of that conversation she'd over-heard in the bathroom that fateful night. Zac Valenti was the *last* person she could turn to.

And her father…

Jocelyn Lyndon-Holt was right in some sick way—*how* could Rose live with herself, knowing she'd denied her father a chance to be well again?

A sense of futility had sunk deep into the pit of her being. And the realisation that through her own choices and actions she was now trapped—for better or worse.

And just like that, without having to say another word, Mrs Lyndon-Holt had had Rose exactly where she wanted her.

With ruthless precision, Rose's father had been trans-ported to an upstate specialised medical facility, where he was due to undergo the preparation required before he had a potentially life-saving and prohibitively expensive oper-ation in a couple of weeks. He'd believed the explanation that Rose had given him: that it was down to the fact that Mrs Lyndon-Holt felt charitable towards an ex-employee. Rose's insides had curdled at the deceit.

She stared out of the car window now, dry-eyed but aching inside. A kind of resolve had solidified inside her once she'd realised she had to see this thing through.

She had been unutterably selfish, believing she could take something that should never have belonged to her—a night with Zac Valenti—and now she had to face the consequences of her actions. And if her father was the one who might profit from it all by regaining his health, then that would have to be the thing that would make this worthwhile.

That and the new life growing in her belly. A life that she would never regret making, no matter what happened from this moment on. Whether or not her child *did* inherit a vast fortune was neither here nor there, because Rose had never set out to profit personally from the agreement with Zac's mother, no matter what she'd signed.

But she couldn't blame someone else for her own actions.

She just knew she would lay down her own life to protect her baby from any harm, and she vowed now that he or she would not suffer because of her actions, whatever she had to do to ensure that.

Zac's building appeared ahead, and the car drew to a smooth halt by the sidewalk. 'Valenti Enterprises' was written in stark black letters across the steel structure. Bold, uncompromising. Powerful.

Rose shivered.

She'd walked away from Zac in his bed that morning and had taken one last illicit look as he'd lain there like a fallen god, the sheet tangled around his lower body, seductively low enough to give a glimpse of the hair arrowing down between his legs to all that potent masculinity that had sent her into orbit.

It had been a wrench to tear her gaze from him, and an even bigger wrench to walk away, expecting never to see him again. Expecting to hold that night in her memory like a perfect precious secret.

But now there was no hope of it staying perfect or precious or secret. It had been shattered to pieces and she had no one to blame but herself.

The journey up to Zac's office seemed to take a nanosecond. Rose had barely had time to recognise the irony of the fact that time sped up when you least wanted it to, when a smartly dressed young man was opening a huge door and ushering her into a vast office.

She saw him immediately, which caused her to stumble to a stop barely inside the door. Zac was sitting behind a big solid wooden desk. She hardly heard the door close behind her with a soft *click*. His chair was high-backed. All the furniture was big...imposing. He looked bigger than she remembered, even though he was sitting down.

He wore a white shirt, open at the throat. Stubble shadowed that firm jaw and his hair was tousled, as if he'd been running his hands through it.

And then he stood up and her brain froze. He placed his hands on the desk in front of him, leaning forward slightly. Rose had the uncomfortable sensation that he was deliberately keeping his desk between them.

Those bluer-than-blue eyes raked her up and down. His lip curled. 'Do you think you can fool me with another demure outfit, Ms O'Malley?'

Ms O'Malley. Rose's heart had slowed to a *thump-thump* of shock and guilt and misery. Of course he knew her real name now. She felt very self-conscious in plain black trousers and the white shirt that she wore for her work at a small local restaurant in Queens—one of the three jobs she'd been juggling. Her hair was up in a functional ponytail. No make-up.

Heat prickled up her neck and she gripped her handbag tighter in her hands, in front of her belly. 'I'm not trying to fool anyone.'

Her voice came out strong and she sent up silent thanks. She was determined not to let him see how hard this was for her. All she wanted to do was apologise, try to explain. Except she couldn't explain. And the opportunity for any apology had long since passed.

Zac made a rude sound. Then he straightened up and came around the table, and all of Rose's dormant hormones started fizzing and jumping, oblivious to the waves of animosity coming from him across the room. He rested back against the desk and crossed one long leg over the other. And folded his arms.

Rose had had tiny glimpses of this remote man, and they had been downright intimidating. Right now he might as well be a complete stranger, so far removed was he from the seductive man who had bewitched her so easily.

Zac's face seemed to get harder, and his mouth compressed, as if he was recalling something distasteful. 'So, I'm curious…what's the going rate for a virginal prostitute these days?' And then he said, 'That's assuming you *were* actually a virgin? The blood was an ingeniously authentic touch if you weren't.'

His crude words shredded Rose inside. 'It wasn't like that.' She begged silently, *Please don't ruin it*.

Zac stood up and said icily. 'That's exactly what it was like.'

Rose drew herself up, even though she felt mortally wounded. Already. And she was sure that he hadn't even really started his attack. 'I'm not a prostitute.'

Are you sure about that? mocked a small voice.

Zac sneered. 'You're sure as hell no meek and invisible maid either. You're seriously expecting me to believe that both times we met were a happy coincidence, only for you to disappear into the ether and suddenly emerge from under whatever stinking place you inhabit months later, claiming to be pregnant with my child?'

Rose opened her mouth to assert that this baby *was* his, but he wasn't finished.

'You seem to be forgetting that it's common knowledge now that the house where you work as a maid was my family home.'

She wanted to correct him—she wasn't working there any more—but he laughed then, and it was harsh and cold.

'I have to hand it to you both for such simple ingenuity, using the oldest trick in the book—the honey trap.'

Rose recoiled inwardly, realising that he assumed she'd been in league with his mother... And of course she *had*. However reluctantly.

He came closer and stopped dead in front of her, self-disgust written all over his face. 'But your particular brand of honey came with a bitter aftertaste.'

Rose immediately felt protective of her baby, hating the wounding words. She interjected before he could say more. 'I haven't worked there for four months. And it wasn't like that. I swear...'

Zac's dead-eyed look told her what he thought of that little attempt to defend herself, so she closed her mouth. He started to walk around her, like a shark. She stared straight ahead, rigid with tension.

He said from behind her, 'Whether or not you currently work there is beside the point. Tell me—did you get a bonus for getting pregnant, or was it an all or nothing deal?'

Rose's hands were digging so deeply into her bag that she wouldn't be surprised if she was gouging holes in the leather. She refused to turn around, and again said tightly, 'It wasn't like that.'

Zac made a rude snorting sound. 'Assuming that you *are* pregnant and that it *is* mine, I'd say you're still on the payroll. So essentially that's a transaction many would call—'

'Stop it!' Rose's voice rang out harshly.

Zac came back to stand in front of her, lifting an eyebrow. 'Such a spirited defence.'

His eyes dropped to where the bag covered her belly. She was at that slightly uncomfortable stage of pregnancy where her belly was finally looking more defined and less like bloated swelling, and she hated feeling that self-consciousness now. As if he cared how she looked. As if *she* should care!

Rose gathered up her strength in the face of his utter condemnation, justified as it was. 'I *am* pregnant with your baby and I *was* just a maid. I'm not saying those meetings weren't engineered to bring us together...' She faltered then, knowing that however she tried to defend herself she couldn't deny that on some very crude level Zac was right.

But he wasn't even listening. He stood back, arms folded. Formidable and distant. 'As much as I'd love to believe otherwise, I suspect you probably are carrying my child. Jocelyn Lyndon-Holt is so obsessed with the precious family bloodline that she would never leave something that important to chance.'

No, she wouldn't. Rose knew that all too well, feeling sick when she thought of his mother.

Zac's voice was harsh. 'The moment you agreed to accept money from her to deliberately seduce me, you crossed a line that millions of women cross every day in this city. And each one of them probably has more integrity than you.'

Rose fought hard to keep her chin up. This was the least she deserved. She knew that. But, even so, she couldn't help saying, 'I didn't want to do it. I walked away that first night.'

Zac took a step back, incredulity stamped all over his handsome face. 'That was just a ploy to incite me to chase you. To *want* you.'

Bitter gall burnt Rose's insides. Of course he would think that. Why wouldn't he?

'I won't ask again,' he rapped out. 'Tell me what the going rate is for playing God with my life and giving me a child I had no intention of ever fathering.'

The futile anger that had risen up in a flash drained away again. He was right. That was exactly what she'd done. She'd played God. And still she couldn't answer him. Because how could she say the price had been her father's life when that life was held in such delicate balance at the moment? She couldn't break the non-disclosure agreement… If she did, her father would suffer. She didn't care what might happen to *her*. But it wasn't just about her any more.

In the face of Zac's clear hostility all she could cling to now was the fact that she was doing this for her father. To save him. This had to be worth it. *It had to be.* And she had to protect the innocent baby she carried, who did not deserve this opprobrium.

Zac was glaring at her now, silently demanding an answer, and Rose said the only thing she could.

'I'm not telling you anything.'

Zac looked at Rose and the rage inside him reached boiling point. *I'm not telling you anything.* Of course she wouldn't. She didn't want to jeopardise the undoubtedly sizeable settlement she was due when her child—*his child!*—took that hated name and came in line to inherit the Lyndon-Holt fortune.

Zac was dangerously close to the edge of his control, and he didn't like to admit that even before, when his life had been ripped asunder, he hadn't felt so volatile. He'd vowed never to let himself be put in that position again—at the mercy of secrets and lies. And yet here he was, teetering on the very lip of it.

He turned abruptly away from that pale face and those huge eyes and stalked to the window. He couldn't look at her and not fall over the edge.

He wasn't sure what he'd expected, but he'd expected her to show something different from the innocent persona she'd projected both times they'd met before. He'd expected her to be confident. Triumphant. Crowing. Greedy.

And she was none of those things. Or not yet, at least. She just had those huge eyes that looked so damn *full* of something that mocked him for his initial weakness. Because he'd believed in it. In her.

The revelation that she'd used her physical innocence as a bargaining chip that night made him bilious. Her virginity might have been real, but every other moment had been a poisonous fabrication.

He recalled persuading her to stay and those eyes looking at him with such *unbelievable* torment. As if she'd truly had to wrestle with her conscience. And then she'd run, perfecting her act, before popping up again the following week. What an unmitigated fool he'd been to trust that it had been mere coincidence.

As much as Zac would have loved to have her escorted from his building and excised from his life for good, he couldn't. She was pregnant. He'd noticed the barely perceptible thickening of her waist that she was trying to hide under that bag. And he hated that he'd noticed. And that it wasn't having a cooling effect on his hormones. Hell, as soon as he'd seen her photo in the paper his libido had roared back to life.

Pregnant. He was still reeling from that shock and coming to terms with the fact that he most likely *was* the father. He'd never contemplated this reality, too intent on making sure the Lyndon-Holt name died out with his grandmother. As he'd told her years before, she could take her bitter legacy to the grave or leave it to a cats' home for all he cared.

Yet he knew that as much as he might blame the woman in his office right now, and his grandmother, he only had himself to blame, really.

He was the one who'd been weak. His hyper-vigilance had been blown apart as soon as he'd laid eyes on that pale, slender back. Her unadorned beauty. A beauty that would be tainted in his eyes forever now. He'd had moments of suspicion but he'd ignored them, too in heat for her. Like a rabid dog.

He'd arrogantly assumed he had an edge over his peers after everything that had happened to him, but he'd learnt nothing. This was a brutal lesson in recognising his own lack of humility. His complacency.

He'd been the susceptible fool who had succumbed to that sweet, hazy lovemaking in the darkest hours of the night, when she'd obviously—in spite of her inexperience—sensed her opportunity and made the most of it. Milking him so exquisitely with her tight body that he'd not even realised it wasn't a dream because he'd never felt anything like it before.

But it hadn't been a dream. It was a living nightmare. And now his weakness meant that everything he'd wanted to do to avenge the people who had given him life was for naught.

He went still then, as something struck him—a glimmering shard of possibility. A way he could still prevail. As it took root in his mind, for the first time since he'd heard this news the rage inside him cooled a fraction. Because there *was* a way he could turn this around. A way to thwart his grandmother's nefarious plans. A way to avenge his parents far more profoundly than he'd ever anticipated.

By giving life to *another* name. His father's name. *Valenti*.

When Zac felt slightly more in control he turned around, but seeing Rose standing there in his office still hit him like a punch in the gut. Her eyes looked too big. He noted too that she looked as if she'd lost weight, making her seem even more ethereal and delicate. It tugged on something inside him. Unwelcome.

He had to focus. Remember who she was. What she'd done. And try to salvage something out of this mess.

'Sit down,' he snapped, more forcefully than he'd intended. Her slight flinch impacted on him in the same unwelcome place. She didn't move immediately, and Zac paced forward and pulled out a chair, not liking it that she looked paler now. '*Sit*. Before you fall down.'

He found himself pouring her a glass of water before he'd even registered the impulse. He handed it to her and she looked up at him as she took it, some colour returning to her cheeks.

'There's no need to talk to me like a dog, and I'm not some wilting lily.'

With any other woman Zac would have been horrified at his behaviour, but this was *her*. She was as low as they came. He went back around his desk and sat down, loosening his tie and opening the top button of his shirt, feeling constricted. It was time to assess exactly what he was dealing with.

'I presume you signed a contract?'

The colour in her cheeks made something ease inside Zac. He told himself it was satisfaction that she'd decided not to try and play him with some meek little act. Good—he wanted her feisty and showing her true colours. So that it wouldn't be hard to remember the sheer gall it had taken for her to sell her virginity and her womb to the highest bidder.

She took a sip of water. When she looked at him again she seemed to square her shoulders, as if preparing for battle. He told himself grimly that she didn't even know what a battle was yet.

'Well?' he rapped out, impatient.

She swallowed, the movement of her throat drawing his eye down to where he could see the hollow just above her collarbone. He remembered tracing that hollow, tasting it with his tongue... And suddenly the irritation was joined by a rush of lust so intense that Zac was glad he was sitting down.

He hated himself for the desire to let his eyes linger on her. She was beautiful enough to hurt, with rose-gold tendrils of hair escaping to frame that treacherous face. Damn, but he ached to be close to her again, remembering all too easily how it had felt to thrust into that tight embrace.

He couldn't believe it. Even after the worst betrayal his libido had no issues with this treacherous woman. All he felt was pure base need. Regardless of who she was and what she'd done. It killed him to know that his own body could perpetuate the betrayal.

'I can't tell you anything,' she answered.

It took a moment for her words to sink in, and then anger propelled Zac up out of his chair. He paced away from the desk—away from her. Not many people had the nerve to stonewall him, and he almost felt a grudging respect.

But when he turned to her again he just said coldly, 'Can't? You mean *won't*.'

Distaste for everything she represented and her obvious collusion with his grandmother made him realise very quickly that he had to seize control of this situation.

As if she could sense what was coming, she asked him, 'Why are you looking at me like that?'

There was the faintest tremor in her voice but Zac told himself it was just fear, because on some level she had to suspect now that she would not win against him.

'I'm taking full responsibility for my actions. Starting now.'

'What do you mean?'

He looked at her, tightening every muscle in his body against the effect she had on him even now. 'What I *mean*, my sweet, poisonous Rose, is that I'm going into damage limitation mode and you're coming with me.'

Rose stood up from the chair, her bag dropping to the ground, the glass still in her hand. 'What are you talking about?'

Zac savoured the look of growing panic on her face.

'I'm talking about the fact that I'm going to do everything in my power to make sure this baby is not subjected to the Lyndon-Holt legacy.'

He noticed that she blanched, clearly seeing her payday in jeopardy.

'But...but you can't do that. *I'm* the baby's mother. I have the right to decide what happens to my baby.'

Her words impacted on him forcibly.

My baby.

His baby.

He was going to be a father. It was finally sinking in on a very real level.

A surge of something completely alien rose up and surprised him with its force. He realised it was a sense of possessiveness. Protectiveness. And this feeling merely solidified his resolve.

'It's also *my* baby—or have you forgotten that pertinent detail?' He didn't wait for an answer. 'This baby will be a Valenti, mark my words. And I will do whatever it takes to make that happen.'

He read the very definite flare of panic in those expressive green eyes, and saw her hand tighten so much around the glass that her knuckles turned white. In an instant he was beside her, without even realising he'd taken the decision to move. He took the glass out of her hand and put it down, angry at his impulsive reaction.

When he saw how pale she was he had to fight back the strangest instinct to reassure her. Coming on the heels of that sense of protectiveness for his unborn child, it was almost a mockery. He had to remember who she was, and that she was mercenary enough to get pregnant in order to feather her nest.

CHAPTER SIX

This baby will be a Valenti, mark my words.

Rose was reeling. This wasn't what she'd expected at all. She'd expected Zac's anger and hostility, yes, but then she'd expected him to kick her out of his office, telling her he never wanted to see her again or hear about the baby.

Yet now he was saying...he *wanted* this baby? Her initial reaction to that was panic. If Mrs Lyndon-Holt believed for a second that she was reneging on the contract then surely she would yank her father out of that medical clinic so fast their heads would be spinning...

But along with the panic was something else... something far more disturbing... A sense of relief that Zac wasn't rejecting his child out of hand. And that rocked Rose to the core, because she realised she hadn't truly allowed herself to imagine that he would want to acknowledge his child.

Zac was suddenly too close. His scent was winding around Rose, eclipsing what he was saying. Almost eclipsing the turmoil she was desperately trying to hide from him. She couldn't seem to think straight and she took a step back, as if some space between them might help.

Zac, oblivious to the real reasons for her inner tumult, said mockingly, 'No need to look so worried. Thanks to the cargo you carry, your future is guaranteed to be comfortable no matter what happens. But *I* will be controlling this situation from now on.'

Rose felt uncomfortably as if she'd jumped from the frying pan into the fire. 'What do you mean?'

His gaze narrowed on her again, making her skin prickle. 'This is already all over the press, and until I know what I'm dealing with I'm keeping you where I can see you. You're not leaving my sight. You'll be moving into my apartment today.'

She sputtered ineffectually. 'But that's ridiculous! You can't just keep me there. I have jobs. I live in Queens.'

Zac shook his head. 'Not any more. Where I go, you go.'

Rose felt all her blood drain south. The walls of the office seemed to be drawing closer, even though they were made of glass. 'We're not living in the medieval ages. You can't force me to do this—it'll be kidnap.'

He just looked at her with ice in his eyes. 'It won't be *kidnap*, sweetheart—far from it. You're moving up in life… just like you planned when you walked into that function room with every intention of seducing me into your virginal bed.'

A few hours later Rose was standing in front of the floor-to-ceiling windows in Zac's apartment, looking out over the view. She dimly registered that she'd seen it at all times of the day now: morning, afternoon, dusk and night.

Before, it had felt like a privileged view on the world. Now… The windows might as well have had bars on them. Because she was in a veritable prison.

The only thing that had stopped her running from Zac's office earlier, as fast as she could, was the unwelcome re-alisation that if she did he would just find her and bring her back. And also, as much as he obviously didn't trust her and wanted to keep an eye on her, she needed to keep an eye on *him*.

She was afraid he'd do something that would jeopardise the care of her father, and until that operation happened she couldn't take that risk. Not when her father was so close to being made well again.

Self-recrimination blasted her. She'd put herself and her baby squarely in the middle of a bitter battle between Zac and his mother. The sheer enormity of the consequences of her actions was almost too huge to bear at that moment, and Rose struggled to regain the sense of control that was fast shattering around her. As if she'd *ever* had any control over this situation...

'Trying to scheme your way out of this predicament?'

She tensed at Zac's deep voice and marvelled that such a big man could move so silently. She didn't look at him as he came and stood beside her. She was afraid he might see how dangerously vulnerable she felt right now.

'It would appear as if I don't have much choice except to stay here for now,' she said tautly.

The extent and speed with which Zac had set about taking control of her life shouldn't have shocked her. Rose had a sense that whatever ruthlessness she'd seen in his mother was about to pale into insignificance next to his iron will.

'No, you *don't* have much choice.'

Rose glanced at him briefly, but it was enough to take in that gloriously masculine beauty. He'd changed out of his suit into more casual clothes. Trousers and a long-sleeved polo shirt.

She looked away again and swallowed. Her voice was husky. 'Apparently not.'

As much as she didn't want to acknowledge it, because she was sure it was one-sided, she could feel the hum of electricity between them. And a coil of tension, deep in her core, that tightened with every tiny move Zac made.

She could see him now in her peripheral vision, arms folded, leaning nonchalantly against the glass. Exactly like he had that last afternoon. The sense of *déjà vu* was instant and vivid, bringing her right back to a time when she'd been trembling all over with anticipation.

'Why did you do it, Rose?'

His words caught her somewhere between the past and the present and she looked at him, confused for a moment. 'Why did I do what?'

Anger darkened his face. 'You know very well what.' He sent an expressive look down to her belly and suddenly the present rushed back. He looked at her face again. 'Was it something you came up with when you heard other staff at the house gossiping? Did you figure you had a chance to catch my eye? And so you went to your boss with an audacious plan to get pregnant with the next in line to the Lyndon-Holt fortune, scoring yourself a lifetime of idle luxury as a result?'

She felt sick. 'I've told you—it wasn't like that.'

Zac seemed to consider this for a second and then he nodded his head minutely. 'Perhaps not...' Rose's hopes soared for a second—until he said, 'I wouldn't be surprised if it was *her* idea. An idea *you* were happy to capitalise on—'

'Stop,' Rose said, facing him directly. 'I've already said that I can't tell you anything.'

She felt too hot under that incisive blue gaze. As if he was mentally stripping her bare, just as he'd done physically that day. Laying her on his bed, telling her to *'lie down, sweetheart'*, before shattering her world to pieces—literally and figuratively.

Anger that he'd been able to seduce her so easily made

her lash out now. 'There were two of us there. I asked you to protect us.'

Zac's mouth flattened to a thin line and he straightened from his nonchalant stance. 'Don't think for a second I'm not taking full responsibility for my actions. I'm well aware that we made love again without protection, and I will deal with the consequences.'

Rose's hand went to her belly. 'This baby is not a *consequence*.'

Zac looked derisory. 'You're telling me that this baby is more than just a means to an end for you? Please don't insult my intelligence.'

Rose's vision was blurring...with *anger*, she told herself. Anger was good. Because if she didn't focus on the anger she was afraid she might go to pieces.

'This baby is *not* just a means to an end.' Suddenly something snapped inside her. Something she'd been suppressing. It rose up—an awful compulsion to know—and before she could stop herself she was blurting out, 'That night we first met you acted like it meant something...like it wasn't usual for you.'

Zac's whole form went still. His face was a smooth mask, telling her nothing. Already Rose was cursing herself for having said anything. But it was too late. He was moving...coming closer with dangerously lithe grace.

He came so close that she had to tilt her head to look up at him, and she could see the flinty chips of ice blue in his eyes, the darker ring around his irises.

Quietly he said, 'Oh, it meant something, all right.'

Her heart jumped. He lifted a hand and traced the line of her jaw with a finger, so lightly she could barely feel it, but it burned like a brand. She tingled, nerve endings snapping and sizzling. The past was coming dangerously close to the present again...

His gaze moved from her mouth, where it had dropped, back up to her eyes. 'Do you want to know what it meant?'

Rose nodded, even though she knew she should know better. It wasn't going to be good.

'It meant that you piqued my interest—which is exactly what you set out to do. The fact that we had amazing mutual chemistry only made your job easier.'

Rose opened her mouth to protest again, but Zac put his thumb over her lips, stopping her from speaking.

When had he moved so close that his body was brushing hers? Rose couldn't think straight... Zac's thumb was moving back and forth now, over her mouth, and his eyes were on her there. Hot. Desirous.

'Do you know what it also meant?'

She couldn't move. He sounded as if he was talking to himself.

And then he said, 'It meant *this*...'

Before Rose could react Zac had hauled her into his body, snaking his arm around her waist, and his mouth was crashing down on hers. Four months of aching exploded inside Rose as she found herself not hesitating for a second, responding as if the past and present had indeed meshed and there was only *this*...blissful sensation of coming home.

Zac knew that he hadn't intended to kiss Rose for any other reason except to prove a point. When she'd looked at him and asked so earnestly if it had *'meant something'* fury had risen up. She was still trying to play him...

But as soon as his mouth touched hers, as soon as those soft curves slotted into his harder planes and muscles, his motivation grew hazy and his severely frustrated libido snapped and growled, seeking only pleasure and satisfaction.

Rose twined her arms around his neck, hitching her chest closer to his. Were her breasts bigger? He itched to cup one, test its weight and firmness. His hand rose, skimming over her hip and waist... And it was that evidence of her thickening body that finally managed to bring him back from the roaring brink.

Not because his desire was doused—if anything his blood had got even hotter—but because this was only meant to be a lesson, and he was in danger of losing it all over again.

Zac pulled back from Rose so abruptly she was left clutching at air. She opened dazed eyes to find him standing a few feet away, looking at her. Her mouth was still open, fire was in her blood...but when she registered that he was looking at her as if he'd just been reading the paper, not a hair out of place, she cursed herself for a fool.

She shut her mouth and wrapped her arms around herself, hating that her breathing was so rough and that her nipples were still hard, stinging. Betraying her weakness.

'What was that in aid of?' At least she sounded cooler than she felt.

His jaw was like granite. 'You asked what it "meant," the night we met and our subsequent meeting. It meant we had physical chemistry, pure and simple. It meant I wanted to get you into my bed. And that even though I was unaware of your agenda the end result would have been the same.'

'The end result...?' Rose parroted back, struggling to get her hormones back under control. She felt raw.

'Yes. The end result being that *no* woman is a fixture in my life—not even the ones who play hard to get. And not even the ones who get pregnant in a bid to earn themselves a fortune at my expense.'

He smiled then, as she digested his words, but it didn't meet his eyes.

'You're good for an innocent. I'll give you that. Who knows? Maybe you've been practising in the meantime. Maybe this baby isn't mine at all...but you're not going anywhere till I know for sure. And if paternity is confirmed, be under no illusions. He, or she, will be a Valenti. No force on earth will prevent that. This child will not suffer because of your betrayal and greed. It will be under *my* protection, and the extent of your involvement will be negotiated with *me*.'

At that stark declaration—at the prospect of what that would mean—Rose felt fear grip her by the throat, cutting off her breath. She felt weak and told herself it *wasn't* because of that kiss. The sofa was nudging the back of her knees and she sat down.

She tried to rationalise, to reassure herself. He couldn't. He *wouldn't*... But she knew as she looked into that hard-boned face and saw those eyes full of disgust that he could. And would.

Zac Valenti had already shown the world what he did to people who got on his wrong side. He excised them from his life like a toxic wound and he flourished in the aftermath.

He'd famously left his fiancée standing at the altar, subjecting her to public ridicule and humiliation. And that was a woman who hadn't even betrayed him. Rose knew he would do much worse to her.

A bitter dart struck her as she realised that he still suspected the baby might be someone else's. Considering the anxiety she'd endured for the last few months, and the morning-to-midnight jobs she'd taken to improve her father's chances of getting that operation, it was laughable that she would have taken another lover.

Right now she knew that she couldn't endure another bruising round of words or, worse, his taking a notion to prove that he felt nothing for her by kissing her again. He'd done it purely to prove a point. That she'd revealed herself so easily burnt her up inside.

Maybe it was better this way... Better for her to have found out exactly how detached Zac had been all along. Better that than have him guessing for a second how much it had meant to her, losing her virginity to him. If he ever knew that...

The thought made her break out in a cold sweat.

She stood up, locking her legs into place in case they were still wobbly after the adrenaline rush of his kiss. 'If that's all for this evening, I'm quite tired. I'd like to go to bed.'

'It's not quite all, actually.'

Rose looked at him and truly hated him in that moment. She bit out, 'What more is there?'

'Your passport. We'll need to pick it up from your house on the way to the airport tomorrow—along with whatever personal items you want to bring.'

Rose shook her head as if that might help clear it. 'What are you talking about?'

'I have business in Tuscany. We'll be in Italy for about ten days.'

Rose opened her mouth to protest against this further display of might and arrogance, but Zac cut in curtly, 'This isn't up for discussion. You're coming with me.'

She watched open-mouthed as he turned and strode away from her, having delivered his decree, but just before he disappeared he turned again. 'There are some ready-to-eat meals in the fridge, prepared by my housekeeper. Help yourself.'

Rose's mouth had snapped shut, but now she said testily, 'I'm surprised you're allowing me to eat. Surely it'd be preferable if I just wasted away out of your life altogether.'

Zac made a *tsking* sound, and Rose immediately regretted her childish outburst, but at this stage she was tired and hungry and feeling thoroughly claustrophobic at the thought of going *anywhere* with this man.

'I'm concerned, naturally, for your well-being— assuming that you are carrying my child until it is proved otherwise. And to that end I'll be setting you up with the best gynaecologist in Manhattan as soon as we return from Italy.'

He sent a dismissive glance up and down her body. 'I'll have a stylist send over some clothes before we leave.'

This was too much. Hotly, Rose protested, 'I have plenty of my own clothes.' That wasn't actually true, and her own clothes *were* beginning to feel distinctly tight around the midriff. She hadn't had time to invest in maternity wear yet.

As if reading her mind, Zac spoke again. 'While I will be doing my utmost to keep you out of the press until the baby's paternity is confirmed, I can't guarantee their interest will die down. And as long as your name is linked to mine you'll look the part.'

When he was gone Rose sank down onto the sofa like a limp rag. Of *course* all he cared about now was the baby and how she might *look*. A man who dated supermodels obviously didn't want to be seen to be lowering his standards.

She thought of her father then, lost for a moment in all the tumult, and vowed to call him as soon as she was alone in her room. Luckily she hadn't made any plans to see him until closer to the operation. He believed she was working and didn't want her to disrupt her schedule for him.

As much as Rose would have loved to march after Zac right now and tell him she would not be going anywhere with him, she knew she couldn't. For all the same reasons she'd allowed him to bring her here in the first place. And, she had to concede weakly, the prospect of getting out of Mrs Lyndon-Holt's orbit was very tempting.

Rose put a protective hand on her small but burgeoning belly and squeezed her eyes shut, assuring herself that she would get through this. *She would.* These, after all, were the consequences of her actions and she had to bear them. Somehow.

Zac looked at the slim figure silhouetted against the bucolic view. The late-summer Italian sun was glorious, sending out different-hued rays of gold and red as it set to the west. A warm breeze ruffled Rose's wavy hair slightly, and Zac had to admit grudgingly that this was a magnificent setting for her pale rose-gold beauty.

She was standing at a low stone wall—the perimeter of his Tuscan villa which overlooked miles and miles of rolling hilly green countryside, not far from the city of Siena.

Rose was wearing some of the clothes he'd had sent over to the apartment before they'd left New York. The expensive fabrics suited her. Skinny jeans clung to her slim legs like a second skin. Her feet were encased in flat leather sandals. And then higher...to where her pert derriere and slim back gave no indication that she was pregnant from behind.

Even though he couldn't see her belly right now, he had been acutely conscious of the small proud swell, revealed when the wind had pressed her loose-fitting sleeveless top to her belly as they'd walked to the plane at a private airfield near JFK airport earlier.

She'd pulled on a cashmere top on the plane, and Zac

had never before been so distracted by the way the soft material could mould itself to a woman's curves. Or how tactile it looked. His fingers had itched and all he'd been able to think about was how hard it had been to stop kissing her the day before.

She'd curled up on the seat opposite him, her luminous green gaze glued out of the window as if she'd never seen the world from above before. Even after the plane had levelled off to cruising altitude.

He'd been irritated enough by her prolonged wide-eyed wonder to ask, 'Haven't you been on a plane before?'

She'd looked at him and said, 'Yes, but I've never left the States.'

She'd said it with a hint of defiance and Zac had felt his conscience prick. Then she'd turned away again and resolutely ignored him for the rest of the flight.

Zac knew that part of his irritation was stemming from the fact that he couldn't seem to get a handle on her. She wasn't behaving as he might have expected. *At all*. And that made him deeply suspicious—which was no bad thing in light of her devastatingly effective deception.

He took a breath now and told himself that she couldn't get up to much right under his nose.

The surroundings soothed him somewhat…reminding him of the big picture and what was important. He'd been so caught up with extricating himself from his family and forging his fortune in the last few years that he hadn't even contemplated what he wanted for the long term.

Faced with the prospect of a baby, he had to. But it was no bad thing. Because now he knew that this was what he wanted more than anything: for the Valenti name to survive and grow strong again. For it to be recognised as a force.

He might not have chosen Rose O'Malley to be the

mother of his child, but the conniving schemer had handed him a golden opportunity and he was not going to let it slip beyond his control now—no matter what secret plan she'd cooked up with his grandmother.

Rose knew Zac was behind her, studying her. She could almost hear his brain whirring. She'd had a blissful few moments to explore on her own. She should have known it wouldn't be long before he came to check up on his inconvenient *guest*. All through the flight to Italy she'd been conscious of his eyes tracking her every movement. It was as if he was just waiting for her to do something. What, she wasn't sure.

The view that rolled out in front of her was so beautiful it almost hurt. Her father had always told her how green Ireland was, but this looked greener than anything she could have imagined. It made her heart hurt, because she knew how badly he wanted to visit his homeland again to spread her mother's ashes, and if the operation wasn't successful it might be something she would have to do on her own, some day...

She diverted her mind away from such maudlin thoughts.

Her father was in the clinic. That was all that mattered. That was what was making this worth it.

Zac had described this place as a 'villa'. To Rose, though, it was more like a medieval castle. A huge sprawling terracotta castle, with terraces and courtyards and beautiful gardens tucked out of sight, bursting with flowers and greenery. There was even a swimming pool in one secluded courtyard, and it had looked deliciously inviting.

Zac came alongside her now and every tiny hair on her body stood up. She was glad of the covering of the soft cashmere pullover and crossed her arms firmly over her chest.

She couldn't help saying softly, 'This is beautiful.'

'Yes, it is.'

Rose looked at him. While she'd been looking around he'd changed out of the suit he'd worn on the plane and into faded denims and a long-sleeved polo top, with the sleeves pushed back to reveal muscular forearms.

Seeing him like this, against this backdrop, was almost too much to take in. She instantly felt crumpled and inelegant, in spite of the new clothes.

Zac was backing away now, saying, 'Maria has prepared a light supper. We'll eat on the terrace—this way.'

Rose was so momentarily distracted by his tight behind in the jeans that she was almost gone from sight before she moved.

When she rounded a corner of a small pathway edged with bright flowers, it led straight onto a terrace, where a table had been set out with white linen, a small vase of flowers and candles. A rotund woman with a smiling face caught her arm and led her to the table, babbling in broken English.

Rose had met her earlier. She was the housekeeper, Maria. The woman oozed friendly Italian maternal warmth and Rose had found herself feeling absurdly tearful, reminded of her mother. She'd been shocked to hear Zac conversing with her in what sounded like fluent Italian.

He was sitting at the table now and flicking out a napkin to spread on his lap, reaching for bread and drizzling olive oil on top. He looked remote, and as Rose sat down and helped herself to some bread she said, 'Don't feel you have to be polite and share dinner with me. I'd be perfectly happy to eat in the kitchen with Maria.' Whom she was sure would provide more pleasant company and be infinitely less disturbing to her equilibrium.

Zac sent her a pointed look. 'Don't act the martyr. It

doesn't suit you. And I won't have you putting Maria to work serving dinner in two places just so *you're* more comfortable.'

Rose glared at Zac and said testily, 'That is *not* fair. Of course I didn't mean to put her out.'

She clamped her mouth shut, in case she might say something else, and Maria appeared again to put down a platter of antipasto, beaming at Zac like a fond mother.

Zac smiled back at Maria, and seeing his face so transformed knocked the breath from Rose's chest. She'd almost forgotten what it was like to be under that all too seductive approving regard, and she felt ridiculously emotional for a moment.

But as soon as Maria left the smile faded and Zac busied himself with the food. He glanced at her empty plate. 'You don't like antipasto?'

Rose forced herself to take some dried meats and salad, knowing that she couldn't let Zac ruin her appetite. It wasn't good for her or the baby. And, once she'd started eating and tasted the delicious food, her appetite thankfully kicked in.

Despite the ever-constant levels of tension, Rose found that she was relaxing as the evening closed in around them, bringing the melodic calls of native birds. The sky looked like velvet strewn with pink ribbons, and the air was warm and fragrant.

It was…idyllic. A million miles from Manhattan and Zac's supercharged life. Yet, looking at him now, she thought he might have been born to this. He looked like a true Italian, and for the first time Rose found herself wondering about the origin of the break between him and his family.

'What kind of business are you involved in here in Italy?'

Zac put his coffee cup down. It should have looked ridiculous in his big hands, but of course it didn't. It only reminded Rose of what those hands had felt like on her body. She flushed.

Sounding distinctly reluctant, he said after a few seconds, 'It's a mine nearby. It was defunct, but we did some exploration and discovered a new seam of iron.'

Rose frowned. 'I didn't know you were involved with the industry—I thought you dealt only in finance and the hotel and nightclub business.'

He raised a brow. 'There's a lot you don't know about me, Rose.'

She might have asked more about the business if she'd felt she could. But Zac was right—what on earth did she really know about him? It scared her to think how easily she'd trusted herself to him in the beginning. And he'd only had to kiss her yesterday before she'd started cleaving to him again like some kind of starved groupie.

Zac stood abruptly from the table, putting down his napkin, clearly done with their tense dinner. 'If you'll excuse me, I have some calls to make. You should get an early night—you look tired.'

If Rose had felt at a low ebb earlier next to Zac's rude vitality, now she felt even more lacklustre. She didn't doubt that not many women had the nerve to appear in Zac's company looking anything less than stunning.

He was about to walk away when she called after him lightly, 'I presume I'm to be seen and not heard for the next ten days?'

Zac turned back, the lines of his body suddenly tense. 'Don't worry, Rose, I won't forget you're here.'

He disappeared into the sprawling villa and Rose deflated like a balloon, all the tension leaving her body. She hated it that she was in such a constant state of awareness around him when he barely tolerated her.

Something dangerous tugged on her emotions now that she was mercifully unobserved. If only those two first times she'd met him hadn't been so magical...if only she hadn't been tempted to take what he was offering and convince herself that it would be okay...

Rose shook her head at herself. She had to stop thinking like that.

She had no regrets...

She put a hand over her small belly and took a deep breath, trying not to let a feeling of being all alone steal over her. She refused to give in to that vulnerability. She'd gotten herself into this situation—her and this baby—and it was up to her to make the best of it.

CHAPTER SEVEN

FOR THREE DAYS Rose had an almost pleasant time. A wave of exhaustion had seemed to hit her after that first night, and she'd spent most of her time sleeping, taking long siestas during the hottest part of the day. Then Maria had taken her into the local village when she'd gone shopping the previous day, and Rose had loved looking around the market and the small artisan shops.

Zac had come and gone from the villa, sometimes using a helicopter, and hadn't offered to share a meal with Rose again. She'd gotten used to eating alone on the terrace and told herself she didn't mind. How could she mind? She was in one of the world's most amazing locations and she was being waited on hand and foot, like a princess.

She'd braved the pool earlier, and lay beside it now after a long, leisurely swim. She was trying to engage with a book she'd taken from one of the bookshelves in the comfortable den.

That was the other thing about this house…it didn't resemble the ascetic decoration of Zac's apartment in New York. This was more like a home. Rose could imagine a family here…children chasing each other through the pathways and gardens…

She put down the book and closed her eyes, losing

herself for a moment in the daydream, an unconscious smile making her mouth curl up...

Zac stood at a standstill in the shadows of a tree near the pool. Rose was reclining on a sun lounger in a bikini. As a connoisseur of women's clothing, Zac knew this bikini was perfectly respectable—demure, even—but his eyes devoured her slim limbs and high breasts as if he'd never seen a semi-naked woman before.

His body got hard in an instant, and he scowled at his reaction. She wasn't even *trying* to be sexy. She had a hand spread across her burgeoning belly and Zac felt the most compelling impulse to go over and place his hand there too, feel it for himself. Would it be firm? Could she feel the baby kicking yet?

In an effort to try and break out of his stasis he dragged his gaze up to her face and saw her smile. He had been feeling a measure of guilt for having left her to her own devices for the last three days. Ridiculous guilt. It wasn't as if she was his lover and he was here to entertain her. She was here merely because he wanted her where he could keep an eye on her. And she was in the lap of luxury.

Maria, who was clearly a fan of Rose, seemed to think it was her duty to give him a blow-by-blow account of all her movements. So he knew she'd been sleeping a lot. And that she'd gone to the market and had enjoyed it, by all accounts.

And now here she was, with an enigmatic secret smile on her mouth.

Zac battled with the darkness lodging inside him as the insidious suspicion struck him that he was jealous of that smile, of whatever was causing it.

Frantically, he denied it to himself. Why wouldn't she be smiling? he rationalised. She'd hit the jackpot, exactly as that headline had said. She had his baby in her belly and she would want for nothing ever again.

A surge of protectiveness rose up inside him for the child as he thought of Rose scheming with his grandmother. All of which renewed Zac's intentions to make sure his child remained in *his* custody, kept well out of his grandmother's reach and protected from whatever future machinations Rose had planned.

Except right now she looked less like a devious manipulator and more like that fey creature Zac had likened her to when he'd first seen her. Damn her.

As if hearing his thoughts, Rose turned her head and opened her eyes, that green gaze landing directly on him. The smile immediately slipped from her face and she sat up, cheeks colouring. 'I didn't hear you.'

Zac felt like a peeping Tom. He stepped out from the shadows and saw Rose reach for a short robe, which she quickly pulled around herself. It made him say provocatively, 'It's nothing I haven't seen before.'

He saw her cheeks redden in earnest now. How was it that she could still project such innocence when the evidence of her treachery was there as plain as day, expanding her waistline? Which should *not* be turning him on—*dammit*. He put a screeching halt on his wandering thoughts.

Something about that sphinx-like smile she'd had on her face just now made him want to test her. He said, 'I'm going out to the mine to check on progress. You could come if you like?'

He regretted the impulse as soon as he'd spoken out loud. It was no place for a woman—much less a pregnant woman. But she was looking at him now with wide eyes, and something in those green depths stopped him from taking the invitation back.

'Really?'

This was the last response Zac had expected. Most women he knew would run a mile from anything that sounded remotely boring or work-related, but she actually looked excited. His conscience pricked again for leaving her alone.

Far too belatedly he tried to change her mind. 'It's really not that exciting. It's grimy and dusty...'

'I don't mind...but I don't want to be in your way.'

Feeling bemused now, but also wanting to see how far she would go before bailing, Zac said, 'You won't be.'

She stood up and said quickly, 'I'll just go and change.'

He called after her as she hurried off. 'Put on something practical—like jeans and a long-sleeved shirt.'

It was only when she'd left and Zac was waiting for her that he realised there was a little hum of something that felt suspiciously like excitement in his blood. He tried to suppress it, telling himself it wasn't because she was coming with him. He was just testing her. That was all. And he was intrigued to see how long she would keep the interested act up. No doubt she was just seizing an opportunity to court his favour.

But then she emerged minutes later, in soft faded jeans, sneakers and a light long-sleeved shirt, her hair pulled back into a ponytail and an anxious look on her face, asking, 'Is this okay?' And suddenly Zac wasn't sure of anything at all. Except for the surge of heat in his body.

Gruffly he said, 'It's fine, we'll go in the Jeep.'

Rose strapped herself into the passenger seat, feeling ridiculously buoyed up that Zac had asked her to come with him. Well, had grudgingly offered to take her. She hoped, as they drove out of the estate, that she hadn't appeared like an eager puppy, starved of affection.

Zac drove the Jeep with the same insouciant confidence that pervaded everything he did. Fast, but not too fast. Smooth. The countryside rolled out around them, stunning.

Rose said, 'I can't believe there are mines here. It seems such a shame to churn up this scenery.'

Zac's mouth tipped up slightly at one corner. 'I think the local population figure some desecration of the scenery is worth the benefits of having a local industry.'

Never had Rose felt more aware of her education going only as far as graduating from high school. She flushed with embarrassment. 'Well, of course. I didn't mean—'

'I know what you meant,' Zac surprised her by saying. 'I agree—it does seem slightly sacrilegious to mess with this view. This is one of the few mines that is still functioning—most of the seams have been depleted by now. It's rare to find an untapped source of raw minerals.'

He glanced at her then, but Rose kept looking straight ahead, aware of the fact that there seemed to be a very delicate cessation in hostilities. She didn't want to say anything to provoke his sharp tongue again.

Then he surprised her by asking, 'How are you feeling… you know, with the pregnancy? We haven't really spoken about that. Do you have morning sickness?'

Rose looked at him, and then quickly schooled her features in case he was offended by her obvious surprise at his question.

She put a hand to her belly. 'I've been okay, actually. Luckily. I only experienced morning sickness in the first eight weeks, and then it seemed to pass. Every now and then if a strong smell hits me I might get nauseous…but nothing untoward. At my last doctor's visit she said everything looked okay. But I should have a scan at around twenty weeks.'

Zac surprised her by saying, 'I have a local gynaecologist on standby in case you need anything. And the hospital in Siena is only a short helicopter ride away.'

She was strangely touched to hear that he'd organised this. Until she realised that of course his concern was for his potential future heir, which seemed to matter to him as much as it did to his mother.

She still didn't know what had caused the rift between them, and wondered if she ever would. Something she'd noticed in the small local village the previous day came back to her, but while Zac was being civil enough right now, she didn't want to push it by asking him anything personal.

'Well, thank you—that's reassuring... But I'm sure I won't need to use their facilities.'

The rest of the journey passed in surprisingly easy silence, and then Rose could see that the hills around them were gradually losing their greenery and becoming more stripped back. A huge stone entrance was looming, and Zac drove in through a gate, waving at the security guard who tipped his hat at him.

The quarry was grey, the earth hacked and cut into all around them. They drove down a precipitously winding path to a deep ravine, where openings into tunnels were visible. Rose shuddered lightly at the thought of going down a dark shaft deep into the earth.

Above ground it looked stark and desolate, but Rose was fascinated to think of the riches that were obviously mined from the earth. She followed Zac out of the Jeep and he led her over to a large Portakabin office, where he handed her a high-visibility sleeveless jacket and a hard hat, and then a mask to put over her mouth.

She looked at him, and he said, 'It's probably not really necessary, but I'm not taking any risks.'

Of course. The baby.

Rose dutifully put on the mask and followed him back out. He was talking to a foreman and looking out over the whole quarry, which looked like a riverbed run dry when it had really been gouged out of the earth by men and machines.

Zac introduced her to the man and she pulled down her mask momentarily to greet him—only for Zac to scowl and pull it back up. She glared at him, but was more unsettled by the brush of his fingers against her mouth. He seemed to be transfixed too, for a moment, before breaking their staring contest and leading her away from the office.

Her mouth tingled where he'd touched it and she cursed her reaction. What if he did actually kiss her again? That thought made her stumble on the path down into the quarry, but strong arms wrapped around her so fast she couldn't breathe. She was pulled back into Zac's body and the imprint of his lean muscles was like a brand, mocking her for her flight of fancy, because he wouldn't touch her like that again.

She scrambled free, saying breathily, 'I'm fine.'

She was glad of the mask now, feeling her face burn. Thankfully he let her go, and Rose watched where she put her feet from then on.

She did her best to ignore her reaction as they continued their tour of the quarry. Rose was inordinately touched when his foreman spoke in English, obviously so she could understand what he was saying. And everyone they saw greeted Zac with a deference more suited to a visiting dignitary.

When she lagged behind at one point, looking down one of the cavernous shafts with a kind of dread fascination, another man in a suit stopped to wait for her. He asked her some polite questions and then confided with obvious awe,

'This region was dying a slow death until Signor Valenti came back and invested in the mine. We all knew there was a possibility of more seams, but he was the only one who cared enough to invest. It was a huge gamble, but it's paid off and we have him to thank for it.'

The man was called away by someone before he could continue, and now Rose was more intrigued than ever. What on earth would have induced Zac to take a gamble on investing in a mine in deepest Tuscany when the industry had all but died out?

He was striding back towards her now, and Rose's heart swooped. Even against this barren backdrop, with a hard hat on his head, he looked vital and disgustingly handsome.

'I'm done here. We can go now.'

Rose looked at her watch and was surprised to see that a couple of hours had passed. She'd been more engrossed than she'd thought she might be; it was such an alien but interesting place.

They handed in their jackets and hats, and when they were back in the Jeep Rose said, 'Thank you for bringing me. I enjoyed seeing it.'

Zac looked at her and arched a suspicious brow. Rose chose to ignore his obvious scepticism at her professed enjoyment and asked, 'Is this where you've been going since we arrived?'

He looked back to the road, his jaw clenching minutely, before he said, 'Here, and also in Siena. I'm opening a new hotel there in a few months.'

'Wow,' Rose said. 'You're really marking your territory.'

Zac made a noncommittal noise, and then his phone rang through the car's hands-free system. He said to Rose, 'Do you mind if I take this? It's important.'

She waved a hand. 'Not at all.'

He took the call and spoke entirely in rapid-fire Italian, of which Rose couldn't understand a word. She found it curiously soothing, though, listening to Zac's deep voice, ridiculously melodic in the foreign language. And as a wave of weariness washed over her she curled onto her side and let her eyes close... Just for a few minutes, she promised herself.

Rose woke to a gentle knocking sound. She sat up groggily and realised she was on top of her bed. Feeling disorientated, she said, 'Come in?' not entirely sure she wasn't dreaming.

But Maria's friendly face appeared around the door and she said in her careful English, 'Signor Zac is on the terrace—dinner in ten minutes.'

Rose gabbled a thank you and Maria left. A wave of hot self-consciousness washed through her. She remembered closing her eyes in the Jeep, promising herself just a few minutes' rest while Zac was on the phone, but she must have fallen into a deep sleep... How had she got to her bedroom and onto the bed?

The realisation that Zac must have carried her...he had to have... *Oh, God!* He probably thought she'd been pretending to be asleep to lure him into her bedroom.

She got up and hastily stripped off her clothes and put on fresh ones, choosing a soft knee-length sleeveless jersey dress in a dark blue colour, pairing it with a pair of low-heeled slingbacks. She washed her face to wake herself up, and put on a minimum amount of make-up, brushing her hair and giving a deep sigh of frustration when it insisted on following its own unruly lines.

Then she castigated herself. What was she *doing*, primping and preening for a man who barely tolerated her presence in his life anyway?

As she walked to the terrace it dawned on her to wonder why Zac was eating with her, and she also realised that the dress was clinging far too lovingly to her blooming curves, especially her breasts, which were tender and feeling about a size bigger already.

But she'd rounded the corner now, and Zac had seen her and was standing politely. She couldn't fault his chivalry.

She forced a smile. 'I'm sorry, I didn't mean to fall asleep like that. It must have been like carting a sack of stones into the villa.'

Zac just looked at her, with something flickering in his eyes that sent an illicit *zing* of sensation deep into Rose's solar plexus.

'It was no trouble at all.' Then he frowned. 'But are you sure you're feeling all right? Is it normal to sleep like that? I was almost tempted to call the doctor.'

Rose's step faltered just as she reached her chair. He'd been *worried*? She shook her head. 'No, it's perfectly normal, according to my doctor. Fatigue in pregnancy can be quite debilitating, but I feel fine now.'

In fact her blood was fizzing, and she felt more alive than she'd felt in months. The doctor had also told her with a wink—knowing nothing of her personal life—that she might feel increased sexual urges once she'd got over the first trimester. Needless to say that had been the last thing on Rose's mind at the time, but now she could appreciate the advice. For all the good it would do her...

Zac poured her a glass of sparkling water. He sat back and took a sip of his wine, watching her. Thankfully Maria came out with their first course, dissipating some of the tension.

While they ate the delicious starter—simple but delicious soup and bread—Rose told herself that she was being ridiculous to think she'd seen anything in Zac's eyes when she'd arrived. It was just her rogue pregnancy hormones and stupid wishful thinking. *Dangerous* thinking.

In due course Maria came back and efficiently removed their starter plates and replaced them with a main meal of deliciously tender cutlets in a light sauce.

As the food restored a sense of equilibrium in Rose, she recalled Zac finding her by the pool earlier that day, and the way he'd been looking at her so intently. Again she'd had that sense that he was waiting for her to do something.

She felt embarrassed now to recall the daydream she'd been indulging in, of a family living in this beautiful house, its walls and paths alive with the sounds of laughter. She hated that he'd observed her in those private moments. Moments she'd never reveal to anyone… And just like that, her appetite fled. She put down her knife and fork.

Not missing a thing, Zac said, 'You aren't hungry?'

Rose held back the urge to be defensive. She'd only left a couple of bites on her plate, and forced herself to be civil. 'Maria's cooking is sublime…but I don't think I've eaten so much or so consistently since before my mother died.'

'How old were you when she died?'

Rose kept her face blank, feeling the familiar tug of grief that never left. 'Fourteen. She battled cancer for four years…'

The truth was that their health insurance hadn't been enough to guarantee her mother the best of care, and even though she'd been well taken care of there had been time spent on waiting lists that had meant her illness had taken hold and triumphed.

Which was why Rose had had such a panicked reaction to her father's illness, imagining the same thing happening all over again…

Zac brought her back to the present. 'And your father?'

Her insides tensed. She hated this ongoing deception.

Truthfully, but vaguely, she answered, 'He's in upstate New York.'

'And no brothers or sisters?'

Rose shook her head, avoiding his eye. 'No, just me.'

'That must have been rough after your mother died.'

She looked at him again, surprised, and said quietly, 'It was. My parents were devoted to each other…it nearly destroyed my father…but he had me to think of.'

Her father had lost a part of his soul when his beloved wife had died, and Rose hadn't begrudged him that.

Feeling raw, and realising they were straying far too close to danger areas, Rose desperately tried to think of something to divert Zac's attention. She seized on what she'd noticed in the village the previous day. 'When I went to the market with Maria yesterday I visited the local church.'

Zac sent her a dry look. 'To repent for your sins?'

Rose fought the urge to scowl, or to rise to Zac's bait, even as a part of her quickened at this chink of dark humour.

She ignored the comment, saying, 'My mother was religious and I got used to going into churches with her, where she'd light candles for different friends' various ailments and worries.' She continued quickly, in case Zac was inclined to make any more barbed comments. 'There's a pretty graveyard by the church, so I went in to have a look, and I noticed that Valenti seems to be a very prominent name here… It was all over the graveyard, actually—easily the most common family name.'

Rose stopped talking when she saw Zac's hand tighten on his wine glass. He was still looking at her, and she saw him pale slightly under his olive skin. Suddenly he stood up, his chair making a harsh sound on the stone terrace.

Completely perplexed by his reaction, Rose put down her napkin and said hesitantly, 'Zac…?'

She got up and walked over to where he stood, facing out over the countryside. Dusk gathered around them, lengthening the shadows. Rose felt as if she'd intruded onto something intensely private.

She looked up at his strong profile. And then, before he even said anything, it clicked. *This* was why he looked so at ease here and spoke fluent Italian. *He was from here.* This was his land. She could see it now, stamped indelibly onto his proud features. That aquiline Italian profile. She said faintly, 'They're your relations… But how…?'

A muscle pulsed in Zac's jaw, but eventually he said, 'My father. He was Luca Valenti. Born and raised here in the village. He worked in the local mine until he emigrated to New York when he was twenty-five, looking for a better life.'

Rose frowned, not comprehending. 'But your parents… I mean your mother…she is—'

He cut in, looking at her now, and said almost accusingly, 'She is *not* who you think. Jocelyn Lyndon-Holt is my *grand*mother—not my mother.'

'But *how*?' Rose couldn't get her head around it. She caught Zac's dry look and said, 'Well, obviously your mother must have been…'

'Her daughter. Her only child. Simone Lyndon-Holt.'

Rose realised then that she'd never really given much thought to why Zac had taken the name Valenti; she'd gone to work at the Lyndon-Holt house shortly after he'd left and had vague memories of the press assuming at the time that he'd plucked it from obscurity. But it was his name—his actual real name.

'But how did your mother meet your father if he was—?'

'An immigrant?' Zac supplied with a bitter tone.

Rose half shrugged and nodded. She was the daughter of immigrants, so she hadn't meant it like that.

He sighed and ran a hand through his hair, clearly reluctant to speak of this. But Rose was too greedy for information to tell him he didn't need to go on. This, she was just discovering, was her child's heritage. Its real heritage.

'My mother met my father when he was hired as a labourer to work on the grounds at the house. She was twenty-one and promised in marriage to a man from a family of similar standing. She was ripe for rebellion after a lifetime of being brought up in that mausoleum and, after meeting my father, she broke off her engagement.'

There was no mistaking the bitterness in Zac's tone now, and his mouth was a thin line. Rose suspected that he wasn't just talking about his mother's experience and her heart squeezed.

'By all accounts their affair was passionate, and my father encouraged my mother to elope with him—which she did. They got married in upstate New York, and by the time they came back she was pregnant with me.'

Rose was aware of her heart pounding with dread, wanting to know more but not wanting to know at the same time, because it wouldn't be good. How else had Zac ended up with his grandparents posing as his parents?

'When they returned to confront my grandparents—to present them with a *fait accompli*—my grandfather, who was still alive at that point, told my mother she was dead to them and that if she crossed the threshold again they would ensure my father would be run out of the country, exposed for not having a proper working visa. Needless to say they cut her off from her inheritance and all funds.'

Zac glanced at Rose for a moment before looking away again.

'My father wanted to bring my mother back here, to

Italy, but her pregnancy was difficult so they had to stay in New York to ensure her safety—and mine.'

Rose wondered if that was why Zac had made sure she had access to doctors and a hospital, and why he'd been concerned about her well-being earlier.

He was continuing. 'Things got fraught. My father was under more and more pressure to earn money to support them. He was working four jobs at one point, and it was while he was on a construction job that he was involved in an accident.'

Rose sucked in a breath.

'He was taken to hospital, but he had no ID with him and he was barely conscious. He slipped into a coma and it was a week before my mother was able to track him down. The shock made her go into early labour, and by the time I was born—a month prematurely—my father had died.'

Rose put her hand up to her mouth, as if that could stifle the shock she felt.

Zac's voice was leached of all expression now. 'My mother was destitute by then—cut off from her parents and qualified to do nothing except be a social butterfly. In her desperation she did the only thing she felt she could do. She took me to them and asked them to take care of me. They told her that they would only take me in and care for me under one condition: if she left and never returned.'

'Oh, God… Zac…'

But he continued relentlessly. 'All they cared about was having a male heir. My grandmother had only had one child—my mother—and my grandfather had never forgiven her for that, so they seized the opportunity to restore the balance when they could.

'My mother left that day and a week later her body was washed up on the shores of the East River. My parents had kept her disappearance quiet, somehow, and her death barely got a mention in the papers. The scandal was simply absorbed into Manhattan society and hidden—like countless other scandals. I was accepted as their child… as if it was entirely normal for a couple in their late forties to emerge with a baby out of nowhere. As I grew up I heard talk of an older sister who had committed suicide, but I never knew who she really was.

'Years later, on the morning I was due to get married, a woman came to visit me—she was an old friend of my parents…someone who had lived in the same building as them. She'd been pregnant at the same time as my mother… She told me everything, and also that my mother had gone to her after she'd left me with my grandparents, torn apart but knowing that she'd done the only thing she could to ensure my security and future. She'd made this friend of hers promise to keep an eye on my progress, and one day, when she felt the time was right, to tell me the real story. When I confronted my grandparents they didn't even deny it.'

Zac stopped talking, and Rose asked quietly, 'Why did you never go public with this?'

His jaw clenched, and then he said, 'I told my grandparents that if they left me alone to get on with my life, cutting all ties, then I'd let them keep their rotting skeletons in the closet. It was enough at the time for me to take my father's name as my own.'

Rose reeled. She longed to reach out and touch Zac, who seemed so remote, but she couldn't. All she could say was, 'I'm so sorry. Your parents didn't deserve that, and neither did you.'

He looked at her, cynicism stamped into his features, twisting them. 'Oh, I don't know… I had a privileged upbringing, wanted for nothing. Every opportunity was afforded to me. There was even talk of me running for office in the distant future…it was all mapped out.'

His barbed sarcasm grated on Rose's nerves, and she said in a low voice, 'I know that it can't have been easy—or else why would you have left as soon as you knew?'

Zac turned to face her fully and said with quiet devastation, 'You don't know anything of what it was like. The only reason I've divulged this to you is because I want you to understand what's behind my determination to bring this child up as a Valenti. Nothing will stop me, Rose.'

After a long, intense moment he turned and walked back to the table, picked up his half-empty glass of wine and downed it in one swallow, and then left the terrace.

Rose hugged her arms around herself and thought, *I do know what it's like, actually.* She'd lived in that house too, albeit in the staff quarters, and only while working. She could imagine all too well what that cold and sterile environment must have been like for a small child who carried the genes of his Italian immigrant father but didn't even know it.

And clearly Zac saw her as just another part of the ongoing betrayal of his parents.

Rose looked out sightlessly over the moonlit countryside as her hand dropped instinctively to feel for her small reassuring bump. Emotion gripped her. How could she deny this child its true birthright now? After everything Zac had just told her? No wonder he had reacted the way he had to the news of a baby.

Rose had never felt more powerless than she did right at that moment, or more alone. She wanted desperately to be able to do the right thing...but how?

CHAPTER EIGHT

As Zac strode into the villa the following evening, after a day in Siena at the hotel, he was battling all sorts of emotions that had never ruffled his life before now. Primary of them all was regret—for having spilled his guts so comprehensively to Rose the previous evening.

There was a handful of people who knew the truth about his heritage, and now she was one of them. She, of all people, who had the potential to damage him the most.

But he'd been blindsided when she'd unearthed something as simple as the fact that the name Valenti was a local one. And who the hell went for a walk in a graveyard anyway? *Rose.* The woman who remained like quicksilver—impossible to pin down, shimmering and throwing up different facets, and still refusing to behave as he expected her to.

The emotion in her eyes last night had reached into his gut and squeezed hard. It had reminded him too forcibly of that first night, when she'd looked at him with such naked yearning only to run out on him.

The familiar refrain sounded in his head: it was all part of an act. In every moment of those two meetings she'd been aware of exactly what she was doing and who he was. And she was doing it again.

Once she'd known she was pregnant she could have

tried to evade him in Manhattan and sought refuge with his grandmother, but she hadn't. She'd come to him when he'd sent for her and she was here now. So she was canny enough to keep him on her side. Or perhaps this was something she and his grandmother had agreed on... The not knowing killed him.

He shoved away the regret for spilling his guts. He was glad he'd told her how it was. Glad that she now knew he would stop at nothing to keep his child away from the poisoned Lyndon-Holt inheritance. She could pass that message on to his grandmother.

Zac stopped in his tracks at the pool and felt irritation rise when he saw it was empty. He'd looked in every conceivable place that Rose might be. *Where the hell was she?*

Unbidden, the memory of carrying her sleeping form into the villa the previous afternoon rose up. The way she'd felt in his arms—so slight, yet solid, all those soft curves curled into him so trustingly. When Zac had deposited her on her bed he'd stood looking down at her for a long time, certain she was just feigning sleep. But she hadn't woken. She'd just lain there, breathing evenly, tempting him on so many levels that eventually he'd walked out in disgust.

A sharp metallic noise suddenly emerged from the nearby kitchen area, along with a colourful curse. Welcoming the distraction, Zac followed the sound. He was intrigued, because he knew it was Maria's evening off.

When he stood in the doorway of the kitchen it took a moment for his eyes to register what he was seeing, and when they did a ball of sheer heat and lust exploded in his solar plexus.

Rose was barefoot and wearing a loose and flowing knee-length flowered sundress. Her cheeks were flushed with exertion. Her hair was tied back, but unruly tendrils clung to her visibly damp skin.

And all Zac wanted to do was go over to her, lift her
onto the massive kitchen table behind her, strip off that
dress, bury his aching erection into the hot, tight sheath
between her legs and *finally* find some release.

His body screamed with need.

He gritted his jaw hard, clawing back control.

Other things finally registered on Zac's overwrought
brain: a delicious smell of cooking and the fact that Rose
was biting her lip and holding her hand under the tap.
When it finally dawned on him that she'd hurt herself he
was by her side in an instant, taking her hand and looking at the red welt.

'What happened?' he demanded in a harsh voice. 'What
are you even *doing* in here?'

Rose would have jumped ten feet in the air if Zac hadn't
been holding onto her hand and looking at her as if she'd
just stolen the Crown Jewels. Shock and fright at his sudden and overwhelming proximity made her yank her in-
jured hand back and place it under the cold water again.

'I just burnt my hand on a baking tray. I was making
dinner... Maria left me instructions.'

Thankfully Zac was no longer touching her, but he was
still too close and all but breathing fire down her neck.

She wasn't prepared to see him like this. She'd been
vacillating all day between telling herself that she had to
be honest with Zac now, in light of what he'd revealed,
and then remembering the signed contract and its non-
disclosure agreement, and her father...still so vulnerable.

She couldn't trust Zac—no matter what he'd told her.
He hated her so much... Why wouldn't he take an opportunity to punish her by allowing her father to suffer? Even
though deep down she suspected that he couldn't possibly hurt an innocent person, still it was too great a risk.

'Maria left *you* to cook dinner? She usually just leaves food in the fridge.'

Water splashed from the tap onto Rose's dress and she was very aware of her casual attire and bare feet next to his suited glory. He must have been in business meetings…

She struggled to focus. 'I told her I'd look after it— I wanted to try her lasagne recipe.'

She felt embarrassed now—exposed. As if it might be obvious that she'd been indulging in an extended version of that illicit little daydream she'd had, pretending that this was her home and she was cooking for people who loved her. This wasn't her home and never would be. This was just a relocation of her gilded prison.

'Is your hand okay?'

Zac's voice broke through her fevered recriminations. She lifted it out from under the water and could see that the red was dying down to a faintly throbbing pink line. She turned off the tap. 'It'll be fine. The lasagne is almost cooked, if you want some—'

'I didn't bring you here to be my cook, Rose.'

She wrapped a damp towel around her hand and glared at him, hating his effect on her. 'I know exactly why I'm here, Zac. I like cooking and I was making dinner for myself—and possibly you if you wanted it—that's all.'

His eyes swept over her in a searing glance and she felt every particle of her skin prickle in reaction. And then he backed away, almost as if something about her was contagious. No doubt she presented a pretty picture: sweaty, burnt, smelling of food…

'I've got tickets to the opera in Siena this evening. You eat, and we'll leave in an hour.'

Rose opened her mouth to reject Zac's non-offer, but he was already walking away from her before she could respond. And then she thought mutinously: *Hang Zac Val-*

enti. For whatever reason, he was offering her a night at the opera. She wouldn't let him ruin a chance for her to get out and see more of this amazing country.

And as for her ridiculous daydreams of cooking for loved ones…? Well, cooking for one wasn't so bad, and the rest of the lasagne would freeze well.

The fact that this brought back painful memories of the period after her mother's death, when her father had taken to working late in order to avoid coming back to the house that reminded him of his wife's absence, wasn't so welcome. Because Zac Valenti was the last person who should be inspiring feelings of wanting to nourish and connect.

Zac had expected some equanimity to be restored once he'd got out of that kitchen and away from all the delicious smells of home cooking, and the even more tantalising and earthy image of Rose, fairly glowing with a kind of erotic domesticity that Zac had never encountered before.

He could remember stumbling into the kitchen of his grandparents' house one day when he'd been about six and looking around in wonder at this alien place full of delicious smells and people and things. Until his nanny had come and scolded him for wandering off. That had literally been the first time he'd seen a kitchen.

For Rose to unlock some dark, repressed erotic kitchen fantasy was disturbing in the extreme.

He'd only invited her to the opera to shatter that image of her in the kitchen. Anything to put her back in an environment where he'd feel more in control.

But in spite of his best efforts, a sense of control eluded him. Rose sat beside him in the VIP section of Siena's stunning opera house. It had undergone massive reconstruction in recent years—thanks to a major investment from him—and now the roof was open to the elements and the moon lit up the stage as the opera *Tosca* was performed.

Rose was wearing a black silk dress. The neckline was scooped, showing what appeared to Zac to be acres of soft pale cleavage, and then it fell from under her bust to the floor. Short capped sleeves drew the eye to her toned upper arms. On any other woman Zac would suspect they came from hours being honed at a gym, but he knew she'd earned them from hours of arduous menial work. As much as he'd prefer to think of her as being lazy or idle, he couldn't fault her that.

For the first time, Zac had to admit to understanding a sliver of *why* someone like Rose might seize on a chance to get out of her situation. Yet he still hadn't seen evidence of someone who was overly avaricious or greedy.

She'd refused to tell him anything about her agreement with his grandmother, so he had no way to know what she'd been promised. If she told him then he could negotiate. On the other hand, if she wanted to pit him against Jocelyn wouldn't she have told him everything? Perhaps she'd been offered such a huge amount of money that she genuinely believed he couldn't top it?

The circling questions irritated him intensely, because he was a man who dealt in knowns. Not unknowns. And worse than the questions circling in his head was the burning awareness of her. Her scent…those curves, more pronounced with her pregnancy. And this primal thing he felt—stronger every time now when he saw her belly. *Mine.*

It was too reminiscent of that night when he'd taken her innocence…when he'd wanted to brand her, mark her.

It was only when Zac saw Rose clapping enthusiastically, with suspiciously bright eyes, that he realised he'd all but missed the entire performance because he'd been so fixated on her. Again.

* * *

Rose had been so lost in the beautiful open-air performance that she'd almost been able to block out the man by her side. *Almost*. But every now and then his hard thigh had brushed hers, or their elbows had connected. His scent had reached her nostrils when he'd shifted in his seat—which he'd done a lot—and she'd had to grit her jaw to try and stop her body from responding with a fresh wave of awareness and desire. So really she hadn't blocked him out at all.

Everyone was standing now, and moving, and Rose was embarrassed at the emotion that had taken her unawares. She stood and avoided Zac's too shrewd eyes, feeling a little raw.

As they joined the throng of people making their way out to the street, someone stepped on Rose's dress from behind, jerking her backwards. She let out a small yelp of surprise, and suddenly Zac was reaching for her and steadying her, pulling her into his arms. The older man who had stepped on her dress was effusive in his apologies and Rose smiled, saying that it was okay, more shaken by the man holding her now than the almost-fall.

After the apologetic man had left she looked up, heart pounding. Zac seemed to be oblivious to the fact that the crowd had to snake around them to go down the stairs, and that they were drawing more than a few looks.

Her body was slowly going on fire from the inside out…every curve pressed against that hard body. She felt panicky. Why wasn't he moving back, letting her go? He would see in a second how much she wanted him, and she couldn't bear that humiliation again.

She tried to pull back, but he only tightened his hold. She could feel the swell of her belly pressed against him, and then the unmistakable hardness of his arousal pushing against it. Her eyes widened as adrenaline and lust shot into her system.

Zac said mockingly, 'Don't look so shocked. It's not as if you're an innocent any more.'

The memory of that kiss came back...the way he'd looked so cool afterwards, unruffled, when she'd been standing there horribly exposed in her desire. 'But I...I thought you didn't...'

'I think the evidence speaks for itself.'

He moved subtly and Rose almost moaned, hardly hearing his taut admission. She could recognise through the haze of desire that he obviously didn't welcome it. That much was obvious in his grim expression. It was enough to make Rose jerk free and hurry down the steps.

Zac caught up with her, though, and took her hand, keeping her by his side. He said nothing more as they walked through the busy streets outside the opera house to where a driver was waiting to deliver them back to where the helicopter had landed earlier.

When they reached it, after a tense silence in the back of the car, Zac strapped Rose into the seat, his hands brushing against her sensitive breasts.

She bit her lip—hard—and he saw it. He lifted his hand and with his thumb tugged her lip free, rubbing it.

A pulse throbbed between her legs as she watched Zac walk around and take his seat beside her. He didn't look at her again, but she had the strangest feeling that some silent dialogue had just passed between them and she'd made some tacit agreement...to *what*?

She was afraid she knew, much as she'd like to deny it. It was in every pulsing erogenous zone in her body. Engorged with blood and heat.

Anticipation gripped her as the helicopter lowered itself down over the villa grounds, and Rose desperately tried to bring her body back under control. Because she knew that as soon as they got out Zac would look at her with that familiar cool, disdainful expression and she'd have been made a fool. *Again*. No matter what his body might have said.

Zac's brooding silence, and the speed with which he drove the Jeep back to the villa, seemed only to confirm Rose's suspicion that he wanted her out of his sight as soon as possible.

When they stopped, she almost fell out of the Jeep. She was eager to put some distance between them before he saw how jittery she was.

She was almost inside the villa when Zac said from behind her, 'Where do you think you're going?'

She turned around slowly in the main doorway to see Zac standing in front of the Jeep. He was pulling at his bow tie, undoing it and then flipping open the top button of his shirt.

Rose felt a bead of sweat roll down between her breasts. She could hardly breathe. 'I'm going to bed…'

Zac's face was half in the shadows, and when he stepped forward she gasped to see the sheer naked hunger in his gaze. She was rooted to the spot as he came closer, even though she knew she should turn and go.

There was too much between them—too much unsaid and tangled and dark. He hated her. But he wanted her. And she was weak…and she wanted him.

And then he was in front of her, touching her. He placed a hand on her waist and pulled her into him, and the same rogue part of her that had allowed him to seduce her whilst knowing it was unutterably selfish and wicked surged back into life.

And worst of all, as he bent his head and blotted out the world with his mouth on hers, she knew that she was giving in because she desperately wanted to pretend for a few weak moments that perhaps animosity and resentment *wasn't* all that Zac felt for her...

Zac's mouth was on Rose's and he was drowning in soft sweetness. Her tongue was tangling hotly with his, arms twining around his neck. And he didn't give a damn about anything else in that moment. Except this. *Her.* Now.

He knew that if he didn't move while he still retained some control over his motor functions they might well end up on the ground right there, and he'd waited too long to take her like a rutting animal.

He lifted her into his arms for sheer expediency and walked through the villa, straight to his bedroom suite. The room was in darkness, and Zac lowered Rose to her feet and reached for a light. He wanted to see every inch of her. Laid bare to him. He was done with fighting his desire for her.

When he straightened he took off his jacket, letting it drop to the floor. Not taking his eyes off hers, he undid his shirt and took that off too. As much as he'd have enjoyed her doing it, he was too impatient now.

She was just standing in front of him, looking trans-fixed, as if she couldn't really believe where she was. And something glowed in those huge eyes—something he didn't want to see, because it blurred the present into the past. So he said, 'Turn around,' with a roughness to his voice that he didn't relish. It betrayed too much.

But then she did turn around, and he forgot about anything else. Her zip had been driving him crazy since he'd walked out of the villa behind her at the start of the evening. He pulled it down to where it ended, just above her buttocks. And then he pushed the dress over her shoulders and off, so that it fell to her waist.

Rose's hair was caught up into a chignon of sorts. He could see where the pins stuck out slightly, as if she'd struggled to tame it. Something about that hint of vulnerability struck him, and it was not welcome. To defuse it, he pulled the pins out and her hair fell around her shoulders. Soft, silky, fragrant. He wanted to run it through his fingers and bury his face in it… He stopped himself. That was the kind of thing crazy, besotted men did.

Instead, he focused on getting her naked. He undid her bra from behind and pushed that over her shoulders too, and then he came close behind her and pulled it down her arms so it fell to the floor.

He cupped her breasts. They were bigger, more beautiful, perfectly shaped. The puckered pink areolae surrounding the nipples were larger too. This evidence of her pregnancy was intensely erotic. He pinched them, softly, and felt Rose quiver against him, sucking in a breath. He kissed her where her neck met her shoulders and the taste of her skin clouded every sense.

When she turned to face him, dislodging his hands, Zac was feeling feral. He yanked off the rest of his clothes and saw Rose push down her dress and underwear until she was fully naked.

On a reflex Zac went to reach for the protection in a drawer by the bed, but then stopped as the realisation dawned on him that he didn't need it.

He knew that this should actually be making him come to his senses, reminding him of who he was dealing with, but all he could think about was how badly he wanted to sink inside her with no barrier between them.

She was looking at him and he saw uncertainty in her expression. His gaze dropped down, taking in the luscious dips and curves, and one curve in particular: the swell of her belly.

Acting on an impulse he couldn't ignore, he reached out and touched her there, spreading his hand over the swell. It was still soft…but he could feel the hardness just underneath.

An unknown emotion gripped him, making him feel powerful in a way he'd never experienced before—and also humble. For a crazy moment he wanted to drop to his knees and press his mouth to her there, to wrap his arms tight around her… The desire was so strong that it nearly felled him.

'Zac…?'

He looked up and the feeling passed. Lust engulfed him. He gave in to it with a sense of relief. 'Lie back on the bed, Rose.'

The uncertain expression left her face, to be replaced by something more like anticipation. She sat down and Zac put a hand on himself, feeling the drop of moisture at the head of his erection.

But then something dark rose up inside him. He wanted to obliterate what he'd just been feeling and he stepped forward, relishing Rose's avid gaze on his body.

Just when she'd started to move back to lie on the bed, he said, 'Wait—I want you to take me in your mouth. Taste me, Rose.'

She looked up at him and he saw the flare in her eyes, along with that uncertainty again. Every cell was crying out for her touch. The beast inside him roared for full release, but he needed this more right now—needed her mouth on him in a classic supplicant pose, as if that might dilute some of the intensity swirling in his gut.

She reached out a tentative hand and he took his own hand away so she could wrap her fingers around him. He sucked in a breath to see that small pale hand around his hard flesh. 'Stroke me.' *For pity's sake*, he almost howled.

She moved her hand up and down, eyes widening as she saw how he thickened even more. Her thumb swiped over its head, spreading the fluid, and Zac had to bite down on his tongue.

And then, with a quick glance upwards, she leaned forward and took him into her mouth. She was awkward at first, but that, coupled with the knowledge that this was the first time she was doing this was tantamount to having one of the world's most experienced lovers take him into her expert mouth.

She sucked, stroked and licked until Zac honestly didn't know how he was still standing. His hands were buried in her hair. He was a heartbeat away from holding her still so he could thrust into her mouth and find his release at last. But there, teetering on the edge, something stopped him.

He couldn't do it. Couldn't demand that she milk him like this...

He pulled free of her mouth and she released him, looking up, eyes unfocused. No woman had ever looked at him like that...as if she'd got off on it too. He gently deposited her in the middle of the bed, coming down beside her, every nerve and cell taut with anticipation.

He spread her legs with one hand, feeling more animal than man, and explored the slick evidence of her readiness. It was all he could do not to thrust in, harder and deeper than he ever had before, but he moved over her, mindful of the vulnerable swell of her belly that impacted upon him somewhere he chose to ignore, and lodged himself between her spread legs. He forced himself to go slowly. It was torture...delicious torture...as inch by inch he felt her hot sheath accept him and clasp him tight.

When he was so deep he could barely breathe, her whole body arched like a bow against his, and she let out a long, low groan.

Zac couldn't move for a moment. Had anything ever felt so perfect? *No.* And then he started to move, and perfection was eclipsed.

Rose's eyes were shut tight as he lifted one of her thighs, hooking her leg around his hip. 'Look at me,' Zac demanded.

She opened them, and he willed her to keep looking as he drove into her again and again and again. The intense battle of wills was won when she started raking his back with her nails, her body quivering and shaking against his as she pleaded hoarsely for release.

Only then did Zac unleash the demon inside him, and their worlds collided in a shattering explosion of tension that was almost fearsome in its intensity.

Hours later Zac sat on the edge of the bed, looking at the dawn breaking over the Tuscan hills, a faint mist clinging to the earth before it would be burned off by the sun.

He felt turned inside out—undone, exposed. There was movement behind him on the bed and he stood up, reaching for his trousers. He heard a sleepy and sexy-sounding, 'Zac…? Where are you going?' and knew what he had to do.

He'd let his guard down here in Italy. He'd told Rose too much the other night, and this was proof that given half a chance she would insert herself under his skin until she was in so deep he'd never get her out again.

He turned around. She was raised on one elbow, the sheet barely covering her lush breasts. He recalled how it had felt to drive into that perfect heat and feel the press of her swollen belly against him. Predictably his body responded, and a sense of desperation filled him.

'I'm not going anywhere—but you are. You're going back to New York today.'

CHAPTER NINE

THE IRONY THAT Rose was flying over the land of her parents was not lost on her as she looked out of the plane's window. Unfortunately she was too high to see anything of the green island, but her heart ached for her mother and her father.

She'd called the clinic soon after Zac's private plane had taken off and had spoken to her father. The operation was taking place in just over a week—a couple of days after Zac was due back in New York. Her father had sounded in good spirits, and that, at least, was some balm to her ravaged spirit.

Ravaged because she now knew that she'd lost herself body, heart and soul to Zac Valenti. And he didn't want to know.

He'd stood in front of her that morning and every line of his body had screamed regret for what had happened the previous night. Regret and rejection.

And then she'd made it worse, because her body had still felt the bliss of his touch and she'd foolishly thought that she *had* to try and reach him...to make him understand. She hadn't been able to bear the thought that he believed she'd *wanted* to do this to him.

She'd knelt on the bed, the sheet pulled around her, and said, 'You *have* to believe me when I say that I truly never wanted to betray you, Zac.'

His face had assumed that mask of indifference she hated.

'You say you didn't want to do it, but you did. So which is it, Rose? I'm not in the mood for riddles.'

The words had trembled on her tongue. She'd *ached* to blurt out the whole sad and sorry story. To confess about her father... But under that infinitely cold gaze, even while her body had still held the memory of his blazing touch, she'd felt insecure. Unsure. How could he flip so easily between cold and heat? He just wanted her. He didn't *care* about her. And she just couldn't take the risk that he wouldn't care what happened to her father.

She'd felt defeated and had sunk back down. 'It doesn't matter,' she'd said.

Zac had shaken his head. 'You clearly have an agenda here, Rose, and I know what it is.'

'You do?'

He nodded. 'I think you're going to wait until the baby is born and then you're going to pit me against my grandmother. That's it, isn't it? You're going to sell my baby to the highest bidder... But you'll wait until then—until we all know exactly what's at stake.'

Shock and horror had coursed through her as Zac had paced towards her and his expression had grown even harder. Hard enough to strip away any sense of civility.

'I've already told you I'll do whatever it takes to bring my child up as a Valenti. And if that means ruining myself in the process, to pay the highest price, I'll do it. I've done it before and I survived. I can do it again.'

Zac had stepped back then, and Rose had felt the very physical wave of his sheer animosity and hatred. Despite last night, nothing had changed. Things were actually worse. He resented her for what he saw as his weakness. A weakness of the flesh. And her heart had contracted into a small ball in her chest, as if that could offer some protection.

Zac had said finally, 'This is the last discussion we will have on this topic until the baby is born—and, believe me, when it is I'll be ready to fight for custody, Rose.' He'd continued in a clipped voice. 'When you return to New York you'll move into the adjoining apartment to mine for the remainder of your pregnancy. We can communicate through my assistants.'

Zac had gone before Rose had been able to get over the shock of his pronouncement, and his helicopter had been taking off from the villa before she'd been able to find him again.

To say what? she mocked herself now. To say everything she should have had the guts to say before, she realised now. Far too late.

She'd been wrong about him. He was as ruthless as his grandmother, yes, but he was the one with valid reasons. What they had done to him and his parents had been unthinkably cruel.

They hadn't actually killed his parents, but as good as. And they'd deprived Zac of the opportunity of knowing the two people who'd loved him most. All because of their snobbishness and their zeal for continuing the precious family line. And protecting their vast wealth.

Rose could understand now why it was so important to him to be a part of his child's life. He wouldn't do anything to harm this child. He would love it. Nurture it. Even if he would always hate *her* for betraying him.

Rose knew what she had to do now. She knew it wouldn't change anything between her and Zac, but it would give him back his power and it would ensure that their child was brought up honouring his or her grandparents. Their *true* grandparents.

* * *

Reaction prickled across Zac's skin as soon as he walked into his apartment almost a week later. He stopped just inside the door. *She was here*. She hadn't left as he'd told her to. Her scent was still in the air.

He felt that betraying little hum of electricity in his blood that had been missing since she'd left Italy.

He didn't want to see her.

He knew it was irrational, but the memory of her kneeling on the bed with the sheet clutched to her breasts that morning as she'd entreated him had pushed him right over the edge.

He'd still been raw after the previous night. And so he'd told her that she had to move out before he'd even been aware of the impulse. Something had knotted tight in his gut—an intense rejection of her attempt to try and take advantage of the intimacy that shouldn't have happened.

He should never have given in to his base desires in Italy. It was as if she was some kind of a witch…stealing slice after slice of his soul until soon there'd be nothing left but a husk of a man. A shell.

Damn her. And damn *himself* for not being strong enough to resist her. He'd known she was treacherous— he'd *known* it. But he'd had to have her. An unquenchable fire had taken hold that he'd had to douse or die. But sleeping with her had only escalated the hunger inside him.

He'd had disturbing dreams since she'd left: Rose in a hospital bed, her golden hair flowing around her shoulders. Face pink from labour. A huge smile curving that lush mouth. Eyes wide with wonder as she looked down at a downy dark head nestled at her bare breast. Then she looked up at Zac, and a feeling of such wonder, yearning and awe filled him that he couldn't move.

Rose had frowned slightly in the dream, and put out a hand as if to beckon him, but Zac's feet had started moving backwards against his will. He'd wanted to reach out, he'd wanted to go to them…but they'd been fading…and then Rose had dropped her hand and just shrugged slightly, as if she wasn't that bothered, devoting her attention back to the baby.

Zac rubbed his chest absently, unaware that he was trying to assuage a heavy, tight feeling. And then he dropped his hand. *Enough.* This was where it ended and he began to get back some control of his life.

He moved forward through the door to the apartment and stepped inside. Rose was sitting on the couch, and when she saw him she stood up. She looked pale, determined. And even though he'd known she was there, reaction still slammed into his body like a wrecking ball.

'I thought I told you to move out by the time I got back?'

He walked straight over to the living room bar and helped himself to a measure of whisky.

'I have.' Her voice came from behind him. Quiet.

He turned around. 'So? To what do I owe the honour?'

He saw how some colour came into her cheeks at his tone, and then she said, 'I need to speak to you for a few minutes.'

Zac looked at his watch. 'I've got a charity function to attend—can't it wait?'

Rose stepped forward, hands clasped in front of her. 'It won't take long. I need to explain something to you… Well, everything, actually.'

Something inside Zac went very still at the intensity of her gaze. As much as he was itching to get out of her far too disturbing orbit, he was also intrigued.

'My car is picking me up in half an hour. You've got fifteen minutes.'

* * *

Rose cursed her jumping nerves, self-conscious in her jeans and plain shirt. Zac clearly didn't welcome seeing her here, and that had hurt more than she'd thought it would. But she knew that if she didn't do this now she'd lose her nerve. And she wanted to tell him before his grandmother had a chance to get to him. She'd taken a huge gamble earlier today and she had to pray she'd done the right thing, putting her trust in Zac. Her father's life depended on it.

'Well?'

He'd put down his glass and was standing with his hands in his suit pockets, legs spread. Intimidating. Powerful. It galvanised her to put some distance between them and she went and stood close to the windows.

She faced him again from across the safer distance, took a breath, and dived in. 'Your grandmother came to me with the plan to set you up.'

Zac's face darkened with impatience. 'It was either you or her, and to be quite frank it doesn't really matter who initiated it. Look, if you're not going to tell me something new—'

Emotion rose up inside Rose as she choked out, 'It *does* matter. And I need to tell you *why* I said yes in the first place—' She stopped abruptly and took a breath. 'It was for my father.'

The words hung in the air between them.

Zac frowned. 'What's your father got to do with this?'

Rose's legs were feeling shaky, so she sat down again on the nearest chair. She looked at Zac and said helplessly, 'Everything.'

He stared at her, and she half expected him to walk out, but he didn't.

He said grimly, 'Go on.'

'If I tell you what I'm going to tell you I need you to promise me something first.'

His mouth tightened. 'You're really not in a position to bargain.'

Rose stood up again. She had to be strong for this. 'I want this baby to be a Valenti too, Zac. I don't want any part in your grandmother's scheme. But if I'm to go against her for you, and this baby, I need you to match what she was paying me.'

Zac got angry. '*Now* you're willing to negotiate?'

He paced back and forth, energy crackling across the space between them.

'It's *not* a negotiation.'

Her voice rang out, harsher than she'd ever heard it. And it stopped Zac too.

She went on. 'The reason I could never tell you the price she paid me is because this was never about money—'

'Oh, please—'

'It *wasn't*,' she said, in the face of his blatant disbelief.

'If it wasn't about money then what was it about?'

Rose felt numbness stealing over her, cushioning her slightly from Zac's blistering impatience. 'My father is ill. Very ill. He needs an operation on his heart and it's one of the most expensive operations in the world. He was a driver for your family for years. You know him.'

Rose could see Zac trying to compute this information, and eventually he said incredulously, 'Séamus O'Malley? He's your father?'

Rose nodded, feeling emotional. 'Yes. It started a few months ago. He wasn't feeling well and we couldn't figure out what was wrong. After tests the doctors realised that it was his heart. He told me the results over the phone when I was at work in your grandmother's house. Our insurance is basic, at best. It was devastating news, because we knew we could never afford the operation he needed.'

Rose continued.

'But before I go any further I need your promise that you'll take over the care of my father, protect him from any possible repercussions that come out of my telling you everything. He's due to have the operation in two days. If he doesn't have it he won't last until the end of the year—'

Her voice had cracked on the last words, but Zac appeared unmoved.

'Why should I do this?'

'Because he's an innocent party in this. He doesn't deserve to suffer because of my mistakes.'

Zac prowled towards her, his face darkening. 'Oh, so I'm a *mistake* now?'

Rose flushed. 'I didn't mean that. I meant the mistake of letting your grandmother use me as a pawn to get to you, and then everything getting out of control.'

Zac stopped. Even though feet still separated them, she could feel his physical pull on her.

He looked at her for a long moment. 'I'll have to check what you say is true.'

'Of course.' She seized on even the slightest chance that he might do this. 'And then will you help him?' Rose thought she'd get down on her knees if she had to.

Zac was silent for so long that she felt the spark of hope wither inside her... Perhaps she'd misjudged him. He wouldn't unbend. Not for her—not for anyone.

She was about to admit defeat and retreat when he nodded once, curtly. 'If your father truly is ill and he played no part in this, then, yes, I will help him. Now, tell me. Everything.'

For a moment the relief Rose felt was almost overwhelming. And then she registered Zac's impatience. He was waiting for her to speak.

She struggled to formulate her thoughts, aware that she was on borrowed time. 'When I found out about my father I was upset. Your grandmother found me crying in one of the bedrooms. At first she was annoyed that I wasn't working, but then when I explained why I was upset she seemed to get interested...'

Rose knew she didn't have to go into the minutiae. Zac got it. His grandmother had seen an opportunity and seized it.

'She presented me with a plan to go to a function and deliberately contrive to meet you. She spoke about seducing you...getting pregnant...but in all honesty I was so distraught that half of what she said barely made sense. And then, when it sank in, I truly believed that the chances of the plan actually working were slim to none. I have no defence for even contemplating what she proposed for me to do except to say that I was panicking and she was telling me that she would pay for my father to have the operation he needed. She had the contracts and non-disclosure agreements drawn up by the next day... Even as I signed them I knew what I was doing was wrong, but I was so scared for my father.'

Zac was still giving nothing away with his expression.

Rose forged on. 'I spent most of that evening we met hiding in the hotel bathroom. I realised I couldn't do it. It was crazy. I was totally out of my depth. And I was terrified of actually meeting you... I hoped you'd left, that I could tell your grandmother it hadn't worked...'

Zac's gaze dropped to Rose's waist and he said, in a voice stripped bare of expression, 'But we did meet.'

Rose put a hand over her belly. 'Yes.'

He looked back up. 'And then we met again—and not by chance.'

She flushed with shame. 'No, not by chance. But not by my choice either. After I left you that first night I wrote a note to your grandmother telling her I couldn't go through with it, including my resignation. I went home to Queens and resolved to try and look after my father myself, even if I had to work five jobs... But then she came and found me a week later... She told me you'd been looking for me—'

Rose faltered, afraid of Zac's reaction to that, but he remained stony-faced.

She went on, 'She reminded me that I'd signed legal documents and that if I didn't go through with the plan she'd sue me. I was afraid she'd do even worse things, like fight me for custody.'

Zac almost exploded. 'Anyone would know that she wouldn't have a leg to stand on in a court of law if it came to fighting the rights of the biological mother.'

Rose went so hot with instant humiliation that she could feel sweat break out all over her body. And anger gripped her too, surging forth like water from a dam that had broken after too much pressure.

'How on earth was I supposed to know that? I'm a maid, Zac. I left high-school at seventeen with no qualifications. When one of the world's richest women stands in front of you with a signed document, it's pretty hard not to believe that she has the power to annihilate you. Plus she made me sign a non-disclosure agreement—which is why I believed I couldn't tell you anything.'

Rose was breathing hard after her outburst, and realised her hands were clenched into fists at her sides. She consciously relaxed them and tried to regain control. Zac's slightly stunned expression was no comfort. She was shaking from the adrenaline rush of anger and of defending herself for the first time to this man.

But then the expression on his face closed again, became obdurate. As much as Rose wanted to crawl somewhere safe and lick her wounds, she knew she had to keep going—bare herself completely.

She lifted her chin. 'The truth is that as much as she was coercing me to comply with threats of legal action… I wanted to see you again. It's the most selfish thing I've ever done, going back to your apartment with you that day, but I thought…I believed that I could have that moment…that as long as I made sure you used protection…'

She fell silent under the weight of the evidence that all her good intentions hadn't protected her—or them.

As if reading her mind, Zac said, 'As interesting as all of this sounds, I'm inclined to see the fact that you *did* get pregnant as a somewhat calculated part of the plan, no matter how reluctant you say you were to go along with it.'

Rose fought down a feeling of despair. It had always been a long shot that Zac would believe her—but at least he'd listened and had agreed to take care of her father. That had to be enough for now. She didn't see the point in telling him that she'd been face to face with his grandmother that afternoon. He would find out soon enough.

He folded his arms. 'If I do this and help your father, how do I know you won't turn around and fight me for custody of my child?'

She felt incredibly weary now. 'Because I'm putting my father's life in your hands. And I'm telling you that I want my baby to have your name. Your *rightful* name. I'll sign anything you want.'

Zac's mouth twisted. 'I think we can safely say that you've proved how adept you are at *that*, at least.'

His phone rang in his pocket then, and he cursed as he looked at his watch and then back to her.

'I need to go to this function. I'm giving the keynote speech.' He reached into his inside jacket pocket and held out a card. 'Call my assistant and give him all your father's details. Once I'm satisfied that he's an innocent party I'll arrange for his care to be put in my name.'

Just like that. Weeks of agonising, and now the thought that she might possibly have told Zac everything from the start made emotion rise up inside her, twisting her heart in her chest.

She took the card, and he was almost out through the door when Rose managed to get out a strangled-sounding, 'Wait…'

He stopped and turned again. His face was stark. No emotion. When *she* felt as if someone had just ripped her guts out.

'I just…' Rose faltered under that cool regard. She just… *what*? 'I just wanted to say I'm sorry. I never meant for any of it to happen like this.'

She still refused to regret becoming pregnant, but she was sure he wouldn't appreciate hearing that right now.

'I'm not sure you didn't, Rose, but you've told me enough for now. As you say, your father shouldn't be punished for your actions.'

And then he was gone, the door closing quietly behind him. Rose sank down on the couch behind her, suddenly weak as the overload of adrenaline left her system. She was trembling all over, like a shock victim.

The cool lack of emotion in his eyes just now scored at her already raw insides like a knife. The fact that he would never believe she hadn't set out to trap him deliberately, regardless of what she'd told him, was devastating.

In the shattering aftermath of their lovemaking in Italy

she'd truly believed that maybe he felt something for her beyond resentment. There had been glimmers of an accord... But obviously it had just been her pathetic wishful thinking.

But still a tiny bud of hope refused to die. If there was *any* chance at all that she could persuade Zac that she'd never wanted to betray him, then wasn't it worth a try? Even if she had to tell him how she felt to convince him. Even if that prospect made her feel weak all over again.

She knew that if she hadn't fallen for him in the first place—probably from the moment she'd laid eyes on him—then this chain of events would never have happened. It was the fact that she'd wanted him so much *for herself* that had led to this, and she owed it to him to make that clear.

Filled with determination, and with her heart pounding, Rose went into what had been her bedroom and rummaged through the wardrobe until she found what she was looking for.

Zac wasn't sure what he'd said during the keynote speech, but it must have been the right thing because people were coming up and slapping him on the back, making all the right noises and responses.

He wasn't sure what he'd said because his brain was still trying to assimilate everything Rose had told him. *She wanted him to believe that she'd done it all for her sick father.*

He remembered Séamus O'Malley. He'd always been nice to Zac, and had let him sit up at the front of the car when his grandparents hadn't been around. His accent used to fascinate Zac, and he would tell him stories of Ireland and tales of great Irish warriors.

It unnerved him now, how vivid those memories still were.

But if everything Rose had said was true, then why the

hell hadn't she just told him from the start? Of course he would have helped her father. Could he really believe that she'd been all but blackmailed by his grandmother into trapping him with a pregnancy?

All Zac had to do was think of his grandmother's cold, imperious face and one word resounded in his head: *yes*.

Rose's impassioned defence when he'd questioned her intelligence came back now, too, and he felt his chest grow tight. He took this world for granted, but he knew powerful people could be intimidating—and there was nothing more intimidating than the threat of legal action, especially when you couldn't afford it.

Suddenly the conversation around him stopped and a familiar scent reached his nostrils. His companions were looking at someone behind him and he turned around slowly. His eyes widened incredulously.

Rose stood before him in the same black dress she'd worn the first night they'd met. It shimmered and clung to every curve, and to the small proud swell of her belly. Dimly he recognised that it had grown bigger in just the space of a week, and the knowledge made him feel as if something was slipping a mooring inside him.

Her hair was down, she wore no make-up, yet she was luminous. Ethereal. His fey enchantress. *His betrayer*.

His voice sounded hoarse to his ears. 'What are you doing here?'

She came closer. 'I need to say something else.'

Aware of the spike in interest around them, Zac said tersely, 'Now is hardly the time to continue this conversation.'

He saw the pulse at the base of her neck beating hectically and his own blood throbbed in response.

'Now is as good a time as any.'

Zac was aware of the keen interest of everyone around

them and took Rose's arm in his hand, pulling her away
from prying eyes and flapping ears.

He walked her over to a quieter spot and let her go.
'Well? What's so important it couldn't wait?'

She took a deep breath, which made her breasts rise
against the dress. Distracting.

'I need you to know that there was always so much more
to this for me—from the first night we met. The last thing
I wanted to do was betray you...or derail your life... Even
when I knew I was being unconscionably selfish in going
back to your apartment with you that day, I told myself
that you'd make sure we were protected. I thought I could
take a sliver of what you were offering and then walk
away and never see you again. It would be my secret, to
hold tight forever.'

She gestured to the dress with a jerky movement.

'I just wanted to try and show you that the girl you
met that night was the girl you thought I was. Unbelievably naive and gauche. But I was caught up in something
I didn't know how to navigate. And yes, there was an
agenda, but I hated every moment of the deception.'

She grabbed his hand then and placed it over her small
belly. He could feel her trembling.

'The truth is that I fell in love with you, Zac, and I don't
regret for a second that we're having this baby, no matter how it came about, because for me this baby will be
born out of love.'

This baby will be born out of love.

For a second Zac's chest swelled with something that
felt scarily euphoric. And then he remembered... No matter what she said, this baby had been conceived in deception. And treachery. The fact was that she *was* pregnant,
so she could say what she liked. She had him trapped.

A memory surfaced of how reverent he'd felt when he'd touched Rose that afternoon she'd come back to his apartment. It had been like nothing he'd ever experienced before. How awed he'd been by her apparent honesty...

But she hadn't been remotely honest... She'd known exactly what she was doing. And at no point had she attempted to come clean.

Rose had had the last week to think things through, and Zac had to concede that she was nothing if not enterprising. He took his hand from under hers and ignored the way that small hard swell had evoked a need in him to protect. It was a need to protect his unborn child from *her*.

Coolly, he said, 'I don't appreciate this public stunt.'

Rose frowned. 'It's not a stunt.'

Zac lifted a hand. 'Please—I don't want to hear it.'

She took a step back and looked at him. 'You still don't trust me.'

He emitted a half-laugh. '*Trust?* You think a public declaration of love and remorse will convince me to take leave of my senses altogether?' He shook his head. 'You really don't have to do this, you know. It's overkill. Once you sign the contract put together by my legal team I'll make sure you're comfortable for the rest of your life. You've realised that as the baby's father I was always going to win in any battle against my grandmother and you're just switching your allegiance. I get it. I recognise someone bent on survival because I've been there too.'

Rose just looked at him. He could see the light in her eyes dimming. *The light of hope*, it occurred to him, bizarrely, and for a moment he almost forgot and reached out to grab her. She'd gone so pale...

But then she took another step back and smiled woodenly. 'You have to admit it was worth a try,' she said.

It felt as if something was cracking in Zac's chest

Something that had no right to exist. Because it meant that on some level he still had a fatal weakness for this woman and that a part of him had wanted those words to be true.

Ridiculous.

As a five-year-old boy Zac had impulsively hugged his grandmother one day, only to have her push him away so hard he'd fallen and hit his head on a table.

She'd stood over him and said, 'Don't *ever* touch me like that again—do you hear?'

He had to force a smile now, because it didn't come easily. 'It's always worth a try, Rose.'

And then he turned and walked back into the crowd, and hated that it was the hardest thing in the world not to look back and see her face.

When he finally returned to the group he'd been with before and did look back, she was gone.

As Rose packed her things a short while later, in the apartment beside Zac's, she was still in a state of something like stoical numbness. The fact that she'd gone there in *that* dress, in public, and had all but prostrated herself at his feet had meant nothing. Changed nothing.

She'd told him how she felt and it had been like a scene in a sci-fi movie, with bullets bouncing off an invisible membrane, uselessly.

The fact that she'd so weakly taken the opportunity to let him give her an out, by agreeing with his accusation that it was just an act, was something she was not going to beat herself up over now. She had a lifetime for that.

Her child would be her main focus now. And her father.

She took a last look around the room. The black dress was draped across the bed and this time she wouldn't be taking it with her, because it was the last reminder she wanted. Then she picked up her bag and walked out.

CHAPTER TEN

'It looks like she's telling the truth, Zac. Her father's operation is tomorrow. And there's been no other transfer of funds that we can find. It's literally just the hospital costs. We've no reason to believe her father is involved in any way.'

Zac sat in his chair in his office, hands steepled under his chin. With a mounting feeling of vague dread in his belly he said, 'Okay, thanks, Simon. Will you see to it that all the costs are taken care of?'

'Of course—and do you still want to go ahead with the contract you outlined?'

'Yes, as soon as possible.' Even though that made him feel uneasy now too.

'Consider it done.'

When the call was terminated Zac stood up and went over to the window, feeling restless. On edge. He could see the Statue of Liberty. And the Brooklyn Bridge. It was from here that he had overseen his resurrection. And yet now the sense of accomplishment he usually felt didn't fizz in his veins.

All he could see was Rose's face last night, when that light had dimmed in her eyes and she'd said in a brittle voice, *'It was worth a try.'*

When he'd returned to his apartment there had been no

trace of her apart from the faintest lingering of her scent. Even that had had an effect on him. Enough to make him come up with some half-baked excuse to go to the adjoining apartment and knock on the door.

When there'd been no answer the concierge had let him in and Zac had prowled the rooms, as restless as a panther. She hadn't been there either. All the clothes he'd bought her had been hanging up neatly. And the black dress had lain across the bed in the master suite. A mocking reminder of the lengths she'd gone to.

Panic mixed with anger had roiled in his gut. Suspicion had mounted that she'd gone back to his grandmother's, figuring she could battle him for custody from there, but then he'd seen a piece of paper on the table by the door with his name on it.

Zac, thank you for the offer of the apartment but I'll be more comfortable at home in Queens. I'm going to be with my father at the clinic until after his operation, and then, when he comes home, I'll help him recuperate, if all goes well.

As you didn't want to see me anyway, I'm sure you can't find fault with this. I'll be in touch once the baby is born to let you know everything is okay, and perhaps then we can discuss plans to go forward.

In the meantime you can send the contract, or any other correspondence to my Queens address. Rose

Just thinking of the letter now made Zac feel sicker. And he hated it. Wasn't that exactly what he'd said he wanted? For her to all but disappear from his life?

She'd offered him the perfect out, and once she signed the contract he was having drawn up he'd be able to rest assured that his child would be brought up a Valenti. He would have what he wanted and he could get on with his life... So why did he feel so antsy? And why did he keep thinking of what she'd said about the night they'd met?

'I hoped you'd be gone, but then we met... I truly didn't want to betray you...'

It made him remember how she'd looked when he'd first seen her—as if she'd wanted to escape.

And then how time and time again she'd told him she had to go, only for him to persuade her to stay, beguiling her. Cajoling. Seducing.

Disgusted with himself for ruminating on this, and for allowing doubts to fester, Zac turned around—just as his office door opened with a bang and the last person in the world he wanted to see walked through it, with his assistant in an obvious flap behind her.

'Zac, I'm so sorry. I told her you weren't to be disturbed but she wouldn't listen.'

He managed to say coolly, 'It's fine, Daniel. You can leave us.' He added with an edge as his anger mounted, 'I think I can manage my grandmother.'

The door closed and Zac looked at the woman who had shoved him aside rather than let him offer her any affection. She was only five foot two, but to Zac as a child she had appeared a giant. Not any more.

A cold, hard hatred settled in his belly. No matter what Rose had done, this woman was the real architect behind the plan. Ever since her husband had died she'd become even more zealous about the family name. As if she could still try to please her dead husband.

Zac folded his arms over his chest and said, 'To what do I owe the pleasure, Grandmother dearest?'

Jocelyn Lyndon-Holt, clad in a pristine designer suit, was white in the face and vibrating with barely concealed fury. Zac might have enjoyed her agitation if he'd felt more relaxed, but he had a bad sense of foreboding.

She stalked towards him on thin legs and threw down a sheaf of papers on his desk. 'You can tell that little tart of yours that I didn't appreciate her visit yesterday, and that she'll be facing the full might of my legal team if she thinks she can break the contract she signed with me. Not to mention the non-disclosure agreement. Needless to say the press will have a field-day when they discover that she set out to deliberately seduce you for her own gain.'

The dread Zac had been feeling solidified in his gut. He looked down at the sheaf of papers on his desk. Torn-up papers. Legalese language: *I the undersigned do hereby agree to... I agree never to disclose...*

He looked at his grandmother, his brain locking on to one thing. 'She visited you?'

The older woman's too-smooth face couldn't show her full fury, but it came through in her shaking voice. 'She had the gall to come into *my* house and demand to see me—to tell me that she wanted her baby to be a Valenti. She's a romantic and naive fool indeed if she heard your sob story and now thinks that you can offer her some sort of a happy ending. We both know that doesn't exist—don't we, Zachary?'

We both know that doesn't exist...

Zac felt as if someone had just shocked him back to life... Hadn't he on some level, ever since he'd learnt about his parents, hoped that it did exist? Hadn't he based his whole resurrection on some kind of hope for...more?

He hadn't let himself believe in it in an emotional sense—too cowardly after a lifetime of being denied love—so he'd channelled it into his work. Believing that power would fill the gap of *more*.

And then he'd met Rose and the gap had opened again—

painfully—showing him that he did want so much more, and to believe in purity and honesty. Until he'd found out that she'd betrayed him and he'd felt like an abject fool.

He walked around the desk to his grandmother and bit out, 'When did she come to see you?'

She glared up at him. '*That's* all you care about? When you know I can crush you and your reputation to pieces?'

He restrained himself from shaking her. 'Old woman, tell me now—or, so help me God, I'll bury the name of Lyndon-Holt so deep that it'll never be spoken of again or remembered.'

Something of his deadly cold fury seemed to get through to her and she said grudgingly, 'Yesterday afternoon.' Her voice became vitriolic. 'She didn't even want money, stupid girl. She just wanted her father's operation to be paid for. I should have known then she was a useless sentimental fool, and I had my doubts—especially when she left her sorry little note saying that she couldn't go through with it—but then I forced her to meet you again and she actually got pregnant...'

Zac turned to ice. He couldn't deny the truth any longer. Everything slid into terrifying, horrifying place. Rose really had been just an innocent, scared woman. Very naive, yes, but innocent. Dear God, above all *innocent*.

He managed to restrain himself from exploding and said frigidly, 'First of all, she is not stupid. Not even remotely. Second of all, you found a distraught, upset employee and you took advantage of her. You used her sick father's life to manipulate her. And you have the temerity to judge *her*?'

Zac's voice had risen almost to a roar by the end.

Jocelyn Lyndon-Holt's cold blue eyes narrowed on her grandson. No hint of love or emotion. She said disdainfully, 'You really are your mother's son, aren't you? Repeating history all over again. You've fallen for a naive little innocent when you could have had *everything*, Zachary. There would have been no limit to where you could have ended up.'

Zac just shook his head. He thought of himself looking back to where he'd left Rose in that ballroom the previous evening and seeing nothing but an empty space. He thought of the empty apartment and her note.

'You're right, you know,' he said bleakly. 'I could have had everything but I let it go. Now, get out of my sight— before I have you thrown out.'

Rose held her father's hand in hers. Tears blurred her vision when he opened his eyes and squinted at her, saying croakily, 'Roisín, is that you, love?'

She brushed away the tears. 'Yes, Dad, it's me. I'm right here.'

He sounded wonderstruck, his eyes clearing. He looked around. 'It's over, then? And I'm still alive?'

Rose let out a half-laugh full of relief and gratitude. 'Yes, it's over. And, yes, you're alive. You did amazingly. The doctor said you've got another thirty years in you, at least.'

'Oh, now…' her father said, with a tired but relieved smile. 'Sure, what would I be doing with another thirty years?'

She took his hand and put it on her belly. She said emotionally, 'Well, for a start, you'll be helping me with Junior and telling him or her all about where they come from.'

'So it wasn't a dream, then?'

She shook her head and forced a smile. No, it hadn't been a dream. It was a bit of a nightmare, actually, now that she'd have to figure out how best to deal with Zac and the inevitable repercussions from having stood up to Mrs Lyndon-Holt. But for the moment things were good. Her father was safe and that was all that mattered. She would worry about the rest later.

Her father frowned. 'The father, Roisín—'

Rose said quickly, 'Shh... Don't be thinking about that now. I'll tell you about him when you're feeling stronger.' She bent and pressed a kiss to his cheek, then pulled back. 'Get some rest now—you need it.'

It was a sign of his weakness that he didn't push the subject but just emitted a *harumph* and slipped back into sleep.

Rose stood up, her muscles aching from sitting by his bed for so long while she'd waited for him to come round from the anaesthetic. She sent him one last look and made sure all his monitors and wires seemed to be functioning okay, then slipped out of the room.

She was exhausted. Relieved, but exhausted. And, as much as she didn't feel like it, she needed to eat. Ever since the other night her appetite had disappeared, but she resolutely turned her mind away from going back down *that* road.

She'd already set off down the corridor when she remembered she'd left her purse in her father's room. She turned around to go back—and walked straight into a wall. A wall that had its hands on her arms, steadying her. A wall that had a very familiar scent. A wall that wasn't really a wall.

She looked up and her head swam. The wall was Zac Valenti.

She blinked. He was still there. She was very afraid she was on the verge of fainting for the first time in her life and she sucked in a breath.

Zac gripped her tighter. 'Rose? Are you okay?'

She pulled herself together, but she knew she was way too light-headed to deal with Zac right now—if she wasn't, in fact, hallucinating. 'I'm just hungry. I need to eat something.'

With typical Zac-like efficiency Rose found herself sitting at a table under the unforgiving fluorescent lighting of the clinic's canteen within minutes. He had put a bowl of admittedly dubious-looking spaghetti bolognese in front of her and was looking at her.

Tightly he said, 'It was the most edible-looking thing there. Eat some.'

Too exhausted to deal with the reality that he was there, she dutifully ate some of the rubbery pasta and washed it down with water. When she felt a little more fortified she said warily, 'Why are you here, Zac?'

He sat back in the chair, his body huge against the functional furniture. 'I wanted to make sure that your father was doing okay.'

Rose felt heat climb into her face and she said, 'Thank you. The clinic told me that you'd taken over the bills from your grandmother. You really don't know what this—'

'Stop,' he said, cutting her off and sitting up straight. He looked a little angry. 'You don't have to say thank you. My grandmother had no right to take such advantage of you. Your father had been her employee—the least he deserved was help in his time of need.'

Rose had to stop her jaw from dropping. She wanted to pinch herself. Because she had to be dreaming.

As if Zac could read her thoughts, he grimaced slightly. 'Look, the other night...at that function...it was hard for me to trust that you were telling the truth.'

Rose's heart thudded painfully. 'And you do now?'

He nodded, and Rose's insides swooped.

'What happened?'

Zac sighed. 'I was beginning to suspect I'd got it all wrong, and then my grandmother came to see me. She told me that you'd ripped up the contract in front of her and declared your intention to have this child be a Valenti. When I came back from Italy and you explained everything, I didn't know that you'd already been to her. You'd burnt your bridges and I didn't realise it. Why didn't you tell me?' He sounded almost accusing now.

Rose said weakly, 'I went to see her first because I needed you to know that I'd put my trust in you even before I'd had a chance to put forward my case. But when you came back I was nervous...scared of how you'd react. It didn't seem relevant to mention your grandmother once you'd agreed to help my father.'

Zac's voice had a bleak tone to it. 'No, your first thought wasn't to maximise your own defence—it was for your father.' Then he asked curiously, 'What would you have done if I'd said no?'

Rose shrugged minutely, ashamed now of this evidence that she'd trusted him so implicitly. 'I hadn't really thought that far ahead.'

Zac just looked at her for an unnervingly long moment, and then he said, 'When we first met...you blew me away. I'd never met anyone like you. I believed you were who you said you were. And then...I felt like a fool. It merely confirmed for me that nothing so pure could exist.'

Rose felt emotion rising. 'But it did—*I* did—as messed up as it was. And I couldn't say anything because I was terrified of what your grandmother could do to my father.' Rose stopped when she said that, a familiar worry coming back to her. 'Is she going to take me to court?'

Zac looked fierce. 'No, of course not. The threat of my revealing the truth of my parentage was enough to make her contemplate emigration.'

Rose's eyes widened. 'You'd do that?'

Zac's mouth compressed. 'It's time to tell my parents' story. I'm not ashamed of it.'

She felt even more emotional now. 'I think you're right—their memories don't deserve to be locked away forever, as if they did something wrong.'

Suddenly Rose felt very vulnerable as the shock of seeing Zac wore off and she had to contemplate why he had come—now that he knew she hadn't set out to ruin him in league with his grandmother.

He was obviously remorseful, and Rose was still getting her head around that, but he also now seemed to believe what she'd told him the other night—that she loved him. And he obviously pitied her. The mother of his child…in love with him…how tragic. He must feel doubly responsible now, and the thought of that made her feel almost breathless with excruciating humiliation.

She stood up. 'Look, thank you for coming all the way up here, but I really need to focus on my father now. And I'm grateful for your help with the operation, but I have every intention of paying you back. I know it'll take years, but I'll do it.'

Now Zac looked angry, and he stood up too. 'I'm not here to demand payment. I'm here because—'

Rose held up her hand, stopping him, because she didn't want to hear him say anything about responsibility, and quickly lowered it again when she noticed it was shaking. 'Just go—please. I'm sure you're busy, and we can talk about arrangements for the baby another time, okay?'

She started to walk out of the canteen and heard from behind her, 'Rose—*dammit*.' But she kept going. If she stopped he'd see how close to the edge she was.

When she got to her father's floor she looked behind her and let out a shaky breath when she didn't see Zac. She felt a mixture of relief and disappointment.

After she'd gone in and checked on her father one of the nurses came in and handed her a note, saying with a knowing wink, 'Honey, if that guy comes in again please send him my way.'

Rose forced a smile and opened the note, which was curt.

I'm not leaving. I'll be at the local hotel, so if you need anything call me. Zac.

She scowled, even as her heart lurched betrayingly. She wouldn't be calling him. She didn't need anything from Zac Valenti—certainly not his sense of obvious obligation.

But just then, as if to remind her that she *did* actually need something from him—a lifetime of support—she felt a little kick in her belly. Tears of emotion came to her eyes. She'd been feeling definite movements for the past week, but trust Junior to make his or her presence known now—right when the autocratic father turned up.

'This is where she's been sleeping?'

The angry voice woke Rose, and she opened her eyes to see Zac towering over her small cot bed in the tiny family room on her father's floor at the clinic. A young male nurse was fairly cowering in front of Zac.

'Does this *really* look like suitable accommodation for a pregnant woman?'

The nurse went red.

Rose sat up and put a hand to her head when it swam. She hadn't slept that well, and fatigue washed over her.

Zac was down on his haunches in front of her. 'Are you okay?'

Before she could say anything he cursed and stood

again. He was on his phone in seconds, issuing instructions, and Rose saw the nurse take his chance to escape further censure.

She forced herself to stand as Zac was putting his phone away.

He took her arm. 'When was the last time you ate a decent meal or slept properly?'

Rose blinked. She couldn't actually remember.

Zac cursed again and said ominously, 'Right—that's it.'

He led her out of the tiny room and stood in front of her. She wanted to scowl at him for being so dominant and gorgeous first thing in the morning.

'My car is downstairs. My driver is going to take you back to my hotel, where you are going to—' He held up a hand when Rose opened her mouth, and waited till she'd shut it again before continuing, 'Where you are going to eat breakfast and then go to bed in my room for a few hours. After that I'll have a room arranged for you.'

'But I can't just *leave*! My father—'

'Your father will be fine. I'll stay with him.'

Rose's belly swooped. 'But you're busy...'

Zac held up his phone, which admittedly looked as if it could launch a nuclear missile. 'Nothing I can't handle from here. Now, *go*—or I'll put you over my shoulder.'

The thought of Zac touching her and seeing how much she still wanted him was enough to galvanise her into moving. She checked on her still sleeping father and then Zac accompanied her downstairs.

He said sternly, 'I don't want to see you until after you've slept and had lunch.'

Feeling thoroughly bemused, Rose did as she was told, and had to admit that being looked after was seductive enough to be dangerous.

When she did return to the hospital later, feeling much more herself again after some sleep, followed by a long hot shower and food, she stopped in her father's doorway and took in the sight. Zac was sitting by the bed talking to her father, who was laughing weakly at whatever Zac had just said.

They both looked up and saw her at the same time, and her father put out his hand. He already looked so much better.

'Roisín, look who it is! Zachary Lyndon-Holt—' Her father stopped and flushed and looked at Zac. 'Sorry, son, it's hard to remember you're not—'

Zac smiled, 'It's fine, Mr O'Malley.'

Her father went red. 'Stop that. It's Séamus to you.'

Rose's heart swelled so much she thought it might burst. *Danger.* Because what would happen when Zac got bored with this responsibility and went again?

She came into the room and said pointedly to Zac, 'I'm here now. I'm sure you have things to attend to...'

His eyes flashed, but he uncoiled his big body from the chair and stretched—which didn't help her hormone levels. Then he said pointedly, 'A word, Rose? Before I go?'

She nodded and went out with him after he'd said goodbye to her father.

She faced him. 'Look, Zac—'

'No, *you* look. I'm not going anywhere, and this is how it's going to happen. There's a room for you at the hotel. We are going to take it in turns to visit your father until he's ready to go home, and there's nothing you can do about it.'

Rose's mouth stayed open and Zac's gaze dropped there for a moment. Electricity zinged between them.

His gaze came up again. 'I'll see you later, Rose.'

And then he turned and sauntered off and left her feeling frustrated, irritated, grateful...and generally in turmoil.

Over the following week they developed a routine. Zac would do the mornings, until after lunch, and then Rose would stay with her father until late and go to the hotel to sleep. She and Zac passed each other like relay runners in a race. They didn't have any more conversations, but she knew the time would come when they would have to sit down and talk things through. Discuss what would happen once the baby was born.

She felt the attraction between them, but all she could think about was Zac's rejection after that night in Italy. Even if his eyes did linger on her, it didn't mean anything, she was only projecting her own pathetic desire onto him.

Her father had guessed that Zac was the baby's father, but thankfully seemed inclined to let Rose *and* Zac off the hook for now. She felt his shrewd blue gaze on them, though, whenever they were together.

When the time came for her father to be sent home Zac had it organised with military precision. They were driven home in a luxurious people carrier—with a nurse from the hospital who was going to spend a couple of days at the house, making sure everything was set up properly for her father's recovery.

The house had been modified in Rose's absence, to accommodate her father's medical requirements, and Zac had also arranged for twenty-four-seven nursing care. When she'd opened her mouth to protest, he'd just looked at her explicitly. He'd also arranged for a local woman who knew Rose and her father well to come and cook for them, and generally keep house.

Sometimes Rose didn't know which was worse—Zac's

suffocating taking over of the situation or his animosity. She thought she'd nearly prefer it if she was struggling on her own, because she knew how to do that, but then she looked at her father in his bed, in his own home, so relaxed, and she felt churlish.

A week later Zac had more or less returned full-time to the city, but he was calling about five times a day to check in. Rose's nerves were strung so tight that she jumped a mile high when the doorbell rang.

She went to answer it and a courier was on the other side of the door, with a big box and an envelope. When she took them from him he looked a little embarrassed and said, 'I'm supposed to wait for a return note.'

Rose let him come in and help himself to a drink in the kitchen while she went into the quiet living room to open the box. She peeled back the tissue paper to see horribly familiar shimmering black material. She pulled out the black dress…and quickly let it drop from her hands when a wave of fresh mortification washed through her.

She remembered how it had felt to stand in front of Zac and tell him she loved him so earnestly…and the way he'd taken his hand out from under hers over her belly. As if he'd been burnt.

She picked up the envelope reluctantly and a card fell out. She could read it without touching it.

Please meet me at my apartment this evening. A car will be waiting for you. Come when you're ready…
Zac

Rose felt sick. This was what it had come to? He had helped them—beyond anything Rose had ever expected—

and now he would take his due? There was some final humiliation to be had?

She felt angry, disappointed…but resigned. She owed Zac. And if he wanted her to come to him like some kind of sacrificial lamb…in this dress that symbolised so much… then what choice did she have? But she would hold her head high and he would never know what it cost her.

She quickly scrawled a note on the other side of the card and went out and handed it to the courier, who left again.

It was late when Rose was finally crossing over the bridge into Manhattan. The car had been waiting for her for hours. She wasn't playing a game, but the nurse had been a little worried about her father's temperature being raised and Rose had wanted to make sure he was okay. She'd only left once he was asleep and the nurse had been sure there was nothing to worry about.

Her gut was a tight ball of nerves. She was wearing the dress and she'd put up her hair and made an effort with her make-up.

The car pulled up outside Zac's building far too soon, and the doorman opened her door with a polite, 'Good evening, Miss O'Malley. Mr Valenti is waiting for you in his apartment. You're to go straight up.'

She forced a smile and went into the lobby, where the concierge had Zac's private lift ready and waiting. As it ascended her stomach felt as if it was going in the other direction. It didn't help to recall going down in the same lift that first night, and how she'd felt as if she was returning to where she belonged.

She was unbelievably nervous. Her palms were clammy.

The doors opened and she stepped into the foyer of Zac's apartment. Her heels seemed to make a ridiculous amount of noise as she walked through on the marble floor.

The living area was quiet. No sound. He wasn't in the kitchen. She looked quickly into the bedrooms. No sign.

The baby kicked then, as if urging her to keep looking.

She went back towards the living room and spotted an open door, recognising it as the door that led from the apartment up to the garden. Her pulse quickened. She picked up the dress so it wouldn't catch, and went up the circular stone steps.

The door at the top was open and she walked outside. The sense of *déjà vu* almost knocked her off her feet. The air was balmy. The lights glittered. The garden was as magical as she remembered.

She walked along the path and it hit her why Zac had built this garden—obviously for his parents. Her heart ached, but she kept going.

And then a familiar voice broke the silence. 'I thought you weren't coming.'

She looked up to see Zac, dressed in a tuxedo, standing on the small terrace above the garden. She instantly felt dizzy, and her pulse-rate tripled. The baby kicked again.

She put a hand on her belly. 'My father's temperature was raised. I wanted to make sure he was okay.'

Zac frowned. 'Is he?'

She nodded. 'He's fine, thank you.'

Zac didn't make a move, so Rose kept going. His eyes were on her, unnervingly intense all the way. She walked up the steps, feeling acutely self-conscious. The dress hadn't been made to accommodate a growing baby bump, so the material was stretched across her belly even more than it had been the last time.

When she got within a couple of feet of Zac she stopped. She'd thought she could do this—hold her head up high and give him whatever he wanted and then walk away again. But now, in front of him, it wasn't so easy. Past and present were meshing painfully. That first night whispered around them like a mocking echo of what Rose had yearned for so much, knowing she could never have it.

Standing here in front of him with a pregnant belly was the biggest mockery of all.

She took a step back. Too much emotion was rising up. Scaring her.

Zac put out a hand as if to reach for her and she panicked. 'I'm sorry. I thought I could do this…but I can't.'

Zac frowned. 'What are you talking about?' His hand dropped.

Rose gestured to the dress, much as she had the other night, with a shaking hand. '*This*. You want to make some sort of point… Maybe you want an affair for a while… until you're bored and you can relegate me to the sidelines as mother of your child… I know I owe you, Zac—I owe you more than I can ever repay you. But I don't think I can do it like this.'

He came towards her then, with a savage look on his face. Rose only knew she'd backed away when she hit the railing where they'd stood and looked out over the view that first night. *Dammit*, she wished the memories would quit. She was going mad.

'You think I brought you here like this as some sort of twisted fantasy? That I'd get a kick out of seeing you in that dress again and just want you for a finite amount of time?'

He'd put his hands on the railing now and boxed her in. He was so close that her belly was almost touching him.

'You do owe me…' he said then.

'I know I do!' Rose almost wailed it, willing herself not to respond and melt. 'No one knows that more than me.'

He lifted a hand and cupped her jaw, and every sinew in Rose's body pulled taut against her inevitable reaction.

'For the past couple of weeks you've been keeping me

at a distance and I won't have it—not when you told me you loved me. Why are you acting as if you didn't?'

Rose's breath stopped dead. She wanted to dissolve and disappear. This was excruciating. She'd thought Zac was ruthless before, but this...this was sheer cruelty.

Angry at how he was forcing her complete humiliation, she said, 'Because I'm not a masochist. That's why I can't do this...'

He said now, 'When I said you owe me, I meant that you owe me nothing but your trust. Do you know why I asked you here like this? In this dress?'

Rose tried not to seize on what he'd said about her only owing him her trust. It was too dangerous.

'Because you want me to start paying you back... Because it turns you on... Because I embarrassed you when I turned up at the function... I don't know, Zac...'

'You're right about one thing: it does turn me on.'

Rose felt her nerves sizzling.

'But the real reason is because I want to start again. I want us to recreate that night—except this time without any malevolent manipulation dictating events. We're just two people who've never met before. No agenda.'

Hardly daring to breathe or to hope, Rose whispered, 'Why? If all you want is an affair—'

'Your words,' he cut in. 'Not mine.' He shook his head. 'You still don't get it, do you? I haven't brought you here just to sleep with you, or to continue some temporary affair. You're here because you've brought me to my knees. Because everything that I ever believed was important means nothing unless you're with me.'

He wasn't finished.

'I don't just want one night...or a few weeks or months. I want every night and day. I want you and me and our baby—together. And I want that forever.'

Rose shook her head incredulously. Her heart was pounding wildly. 'You didn't believe me when I told you how I felt... How do I know you believe me now?'

Zac was intense. 'Because I trust in that girl I met who was so conflicted...who just wanted to do the right thing but was falling, just like I was. I trust in the purity of what we felt for each other, regardless of how we came to meet.'

It was too much. The hope was too much... She had too far to fall, and Zac had distrusted her for so long.

She broke away and turned her back to him, standing at the railing, holding on with both hands, knuckles white. Her throat ached...her eyes burned. And then she closed her eyes helplessly when she felt him behind her, wrapping his arms around her. His hands spread across her swollen belly with a possessiveness that made her blood sing.

He said over her head, 'I love you, Rose, and I'm not letting you go. Not until you believe me.'

She was crying now in earnest, silently. But he could feel her sobs and he just held her until they stopped. The baby kicked under his hands.

She felt Zac go still behind her, and then he said with a choked voice, 'See? It's two against one.'

As he held her and she looked out over the view, she felt something wild and soaring take root inside her. The past and the present...and the future? Could it really start here again?

She gathered all her courage and turned in his arms and looked up. Her face had to be ravaged from her tears, but she didn't care. She looked, deep into those blue eyes, and saw nothing but a blazing truth, as if he could burn it into her with sheer will. And a question. Could she give them another chance? Could she trust him?

Rose tugged free of Zac's hold and stepped back. The

stark pain she saw in his eyes when she broke free told her everything. And that she never wanted to see it again.

She took a deep, not entirely stable breath and held out her hand. 'I'm Rose O'Malley—nice to meet you.'

Zac's eyes flashed with something fierce. Relief. *Joy.* And love. He smiled and took her hand. 'Zac Valenti—nice to meet you too.' Then he cocked his head on one side. 'With a name and colouring like that you must be Irish?'

Her heart felt as if it would explode in her chest, but she answered, 'My parents emigrated here before I was born.'

Zac kept hold of her hand and slowly started pulling her towards him. 'Why haven't I seen you around before?'

Rose smiled tremulously and let herself be pulled. 'I'm from Queens, and I'm afraid I'm just a humble maid.'

Zac pulled her right into his body and said, in a suspiciously choked-sounding voice, 'As it happens, *just* humble maids are some of my favourite people.' He threaded a hand through Rose's hair, 'Would you think it very forward of me if I kissed you, even though we've only just met?'

Rose's voice wobbled even more as she said emotionally, 'Only as long as you promise never to stop.'

'That,' Zac said reverently as he bent his head towards hers, 'I can promise.'

And so that night, on a beautiful rooftop, in the middle of a magical garden high in the dark velvet sky, they started again.

EPILOGUE

A year later

ZAC VALENTI LOOKED around the massive glittering ball-room from his antisocial location, leaning against a pillar at the back of the room. Women passed him, dripping in jewels. He held in a scowl. And then something caught his peripheral vision and he looked to his right to see a bright flame of gold and green approaching him. Something swelled in his chest. His wife, his *love*, his world.

She emerged from the crowd, smiling at him. Her hair was swept up and she wore a shimmering strapless column of emerald-green that made her eyes pop out like two jewels. The only jewels she needed. Apart from her wedding rings.

When she reached his side Zac pulled her in close and it felt as it always did—as if a part of him was slotting back into place. He automatically breathed easier.

Rose looked up at him, eyes sparkling. 'The gossip in the powder room tonight is about the sudden decision of a certain Jocelyn Lyndon-Holt to go on a long worldwide cruise.'

A familiar tension came into Zac's muscles at the mention of that woman, but also a sense of release. He'd given a recent exclusive interview to a financial magazine, finally revealing the truth of his parentage and details of his hitherto less well-known Italian business concerns.

This cruise was his grandmother's attempt to escape her fall from grace. The fact that she would be hounded by reporters at every stop along her route was inordinately satisfying. As was the legal agreement he'd made her sign before she'd left, which had been her only chance of ensuring the Lyndon-Holt name would live forever.

The Lyndon-Holt fortune was to become a philanthropic foundation, with one of its main recipients being a new charity—set up by him and Rose—which allocated funds for expensive medical operations to those who couldn't afford it.

Rose's father had recovered fully from his operation, and they'd taken an emotional trip back to Ireland with her mother's ashes shortly after their daughter's birth. Needless to say, Simona May Valenti—named for her paternal grandmother with the Italian spelling, and maternal grandmother—was the apple of her doting grandfather's eye.

They'd christened her three months previously, in the church near the graveyard where Zac's ancestors were buried. It was also where they'd been married, before Simona's birth. Italy was their second home now, and they retreated there as much as possible.

Zac said now, with faux gravity, 'Quite frankly, I'm less interested in idle gossip and far more interested in seeing how quickly I can get you out of that dress, Mrs Valenti.'

Rose slipped her arms around his waist, pressing so close that he could feel the thrust of her breasts against this side. Lust shot through his system with predictable force, making his body respond.

'Witch...' he growled, and she smiled, well aware of her effect on him.

He pulled her around in front of him, as much to disguise his body's reaction as to torture her a little too.

He smiled when he saw her cheeks flush and her eyes dilate. 'What do you say to going somewhere a little less... stuffy?'

She smiled. 'I say yes.'

And then they both became aware of a moment of *déjà vu* at the same time—recalling that first night when he'd said those same words,

Rose said more huskily, 'Take me home, Zac.'

So he did.

They went home to their new Greenwich Village townhouse and, after sending their nanny home, checked on their peacefully sleeping baby daughter, legs and arms spread wide in abandon.

Zac stood looking down at her for a long time. It scared him sometimes, recognising how easily his life might have remained an arid wasteland, only feeling a desire for retribution for his parents and wanting to accumulate more wealth and power. He'd arrogantly assumed when he'd walked away from his family that he had it all figured out, when in fact he'd really been no better off.

It had taken meeting Rose and falling in love to show him the true meaning of wealth. And now his daughter had compounded that a thousandfold.

Rose's hand slipped into his and he looked at her, too overcome to say anything for a moment. She smiled, and he could see everything he was feeling mirrored in those green eyes.

'I know,' she said softly. 'Me, too.'

And then she started backing out of the room, pulling

him with her, with a knowing and very feminine smile on her face as they made their way to their bedroom.

And in that private space Zac let her take him apart—because he knew that she was the only one who could put him back together again. For ever.

* * * * *

If you enjoyed this story, check out these other great reads from Abby Green
AWAKENED BY HER DESERT CAPTOR
AN HEIR FIT FOR A KING
THE BRIDE FONSECA NEEDS
FONSECA'S FURY
Available now!

Don't miss Lynne Graham's 100th book!
BOUGHT FOR THE GREEK'S REVENGE
Also available this month.

Lynne Graham has sold 35 million books!

To settle a debt, she'll have to become his mistress...

Nikolai Drakos is determined to have his revenge against th
man who destroyed his sister. So stealing his enemy's
intended fiancé seems like the perfect solution! Until Nikola
discovers that woman is Ella Davies...

*Read on for a tantalising excerpt from
Lynne Graham's 100th book,*

BOUGHT FOR THE GREEK'S REVENGE

'Mistress,' Nikolai slotted in cool as ice.

Shock had welded Ella's tongue to the roof of her mouth becau
he was sexually propositioning her and nothing could have prepare
her for that. She wasn't drop-dead gorgeous... *he* was! Male hea
didn't swivel when Ella walked down the street because she ha
neither the length of leg nor the curves usually deemed necessa
to attract such attention. Why on earth could he be making *her* su
an offer?

'But we don't even know each other,' she framed dazedly. 'You'
a stranger...'

'If you live with me I won't be a stranger for long,' Nikolai pointed out with monumental calm. And the very sound of that inhuman calm and cool forced her to flip round and settle distraught eyes on his lean darkly handsome face.

'You can't be serious about this!'

'I assure you that I am deadly serious. Move in and I'll forget your family's debts.'

'But it's a *crazy* idea!' she gasped.

'It's not crazy to me,' Nikolai asserted. 'When I want anything, I go after it hard and fast.'

Her lashes dipped. Did he want her like that? Enough to track her down, buy up her father's debts, and try and buy rights to her and her body along with those debts? The very idea of that made her dizzy and plunged her brain into even greater turmoil. 'It's immoral... it's blackmail.'

'It's definitely *not* blackmail. I'm giving you the benefit of a choice you didn't have before I came through that door,' Nikolai Drakos added with a glittering cool. 'That choice is yours to make.'

'Like hell it is!' Ella fired back. 'It's a complete cheat of a supposed offer!'

Nikolai sent her a gleaming sideways glance. 'No the real cheat was you kissing me the way you did last year and then saying no and acting as if I had grossly insulted you,' he murmured with lethal quietness.

'You *did* insult me!' Ella flung back, her cheeks hot as fire while she wondered if her refusal that night had started off his whole chain of action. What else could possibly be driving him?

Nikolai straightened lazily as he opened the door. 'If you take offence that easily, maybe it's just as well that the answer is no.'

MILLS & BOON®

AOR